The Untold Love Story

Sharon C. Jenkins

Philip Balonwu

Printed in the United States of America

First Printing, 2023

ISBN: 978-1-7354642-3-7

Sunshine Reigns Publishing Company

Houston, TX

(A subsidiary of The Master Communicator's Writing Services)

www.mcwritingservices.com

Library of Congress Control Number: 2023900441

To my granddaughters and their generation, a virtuous seed lies dormant inside of you. Cultivate it and watch God perform miracles on your behalf.

TABLE OF CONTENTS

PROLOGUE

The sun reigned high in the sky on that midsummer day in late April. There was a sense of urgency in the air to find a big tree with large branches and the shade that accompanied them. Buzzards expertly circled in the sky looking for their next prey while two small male figures anxiously made their way to the top of the hill. One as black as midnight and the other as pale as snow. The boys sweated profusely as they intentionally made their way through the brush to their destination. At birth, one instantly became the prince of the northern African dynasty, Dala, a land that was saturated with black gold, and the other, a missionary's son whose life was built on the solid rock teachings of the Bible. One believed in the African gods of his forefathers such as Aje 'Shaluga, Babalu 'Aye', Obatala, Tsumbura, and Ogun. But the other possessed the monotheistic viewpoint of his father.

Dala Dynasty was a commercialized industrialized kingdom known for its magnificent iron and dye work. Located strategically near the Jakara

River in the Savanna region of Nigeria, this mysterious kingdom sat in a dried-up river basin and is flush with unique vegetation and forests. Tall, thick-stemmed trees populated and provided canopies for the kingdom's inhabitants coupled with a huge masterfully built wall surrounding the city that added protection and privacy. Stepping behind that wall was like taking a trip in a time capsule back to the 19th century.

Ezra Sr. was visiting the kingdom for the summer as a missionary to build churches and schools in the surrounding villages for the king of Dala. He came from a long line of missionaries that loved the African continent. Even though he had chosen construction instead of ministry for a career, he purposed to honor the tradition by donating his services each summer as assigned by an international missionary overseeing organization based in the United States from the Baptist World Alliance.

Oba Musumbi on the other hand, was a wise, Stanford-educated MBA, who loved his people and was devoted to improving the quality of their lives. He embodied the leadership style of his father who came before him and held his nation, the people, the land, and their history in the utmost regard. His lifelong mission was to modernize his nation to be competitive in the global marketplace. He used his degree and acumen as a keen businessman to solidify the kingdom's wealth. As a result, there was currently peace in the land. But that was not always the case. Religion had divided the dynasty, and Dalo remained predominately influenced by Christianity even in this heavily populated Muslim region after the conversion of his father in his early twenties.

He especially loved his oldest son Oba Jaiye of Dala Dynasty to a fault. The palace servants had a running commentary on the numerous presents the young prince received on a daily basis. He would often remind Oba Jaiye and anyone who would listen of his rich heritage which started with Bagauda, son of Bawo and grandson of the mythical hero, Bayajidda, the first king of Kano. This steady reminder only fueled his desire to rule his father's dynasty. Oba Jaiye was an impetuous boy who couldn't wait to sit on the throne as king. He envisioned himself as ruler of the palace compound, and his father, the king, indulged him. Ezra, on the other hand, still grieved the death of his dear mother and hadn't wanted to take the trip to this mysterious foreign land. His father felt compelled to bring him along because he wanted to keep a close eye on his son. Both boys had a tendency for mischief and should have required close supervision, but everyone was busy building the kingdom and often unavailable. So, the boys were often left to their own devices and broad imagination.

Earlier in the summer there was a fight between the missionary's son and several older boys in the palace compound. Even though he had grit, Ezra Sr. wasn't a match for the five older boys that attacked him. The young prince had compassion for the boy and rescued him from a beating that could have ended his and his father's stay. All of the kingdom, both young and old were afraid of the young prince because he literally could have them put to death immediately for any kind of perceived transgression that happened within the palace compound. Word traveled fast that the missionary's son was a guest of the prince, and he should be honored as such.

This was the beginning of a great friendship, but as the summer quickly came to an end, so was the boy's visit. Frantic about how to maintain their bromance across the vast Atlantic Ocean, they decided to make a trip to the mountain that housed the altars of the gods worshipped by the natives to solidify their relationship.

They were not deterred by the heat, the scavengers, or the possibility of trespassing against the ferocious gods of the Yoruba people. These things were simply a backdrop to a higher calling. This would be the day that they would deliberately defy all societal norms and cross-cultural lines that spanned nations... today they would become blood brothers forever.

They had grown so close to each other that the king had agreed to let Ezra Sr. share a bunk bed in the prince's palace bedroom. Each night their ritual was to take turns telling each other bedtime stories. Oba

Jaiye shared the stories that he had heard at the feet of the learned griots of his compound, and Ezra Sr. the stories of the Bible. It was Ezra's turn to share on the previous night, and he chose the story of Jonathan and David's establishing a blood covenant declaring their infinite brotherhood and love, honor, and respect for one another. The prince was intrigued with the story because he was very familiar with the concept of blood covenants and their importance. He had witnessed the ceremonial treaties his father formed with neighboring countries and valued this new experience, especially with his new friend that was more like a brother to him than anyone else. It was also an opportunity to use the Arabian silver dagger with the gold crusted handle that his father awarded to him during his rite of passage ceremony. Once Ezra saw the dagger, they unanimously agreed that it was the only pathway for them to stay friends forever, regardless of their geographical location. They decided to draw up a written covenant expressing the terms of their brotherhood. Each signed it with his boy-like scrawl, shook hands, and returned to their covers anxious for their midday journey to the high holy place where worshippers gathered to pay homage to their gods.

Reaching their destination after an arduous climb, each boy fell to the ground weary of their climb. The sun soon reminded them of who was boss, and they found the internal fortitude to complete the task at hand. Oba Jaiye was the first to stand, reaching out for his friend, he quickly pulled him to his feet. Their eyes met.

"Are you ready, Ezra?"

"Yes."

"No regrets?"

"No."

Ezra extended his arm as a sign of his bravery. The prince then pulled out the ceremonial dagger that would solidify their covenant and change their lives and that of future generations forever. And the gods smiled.

THE YORUBA CULTURE

THE HEARTBEAT OF THE DALA DYNASTY

*Y*oruba culture is one of the most prominent and influential cultures in Nigeria. The Yoruba people are an ethnic group that is primarily found in the southwestern region of Nigeria, but their influence can be found throughout the country. The culture is known for its rich tradition, deep spirituality, and strong sense of community.

Growing up as a Yoruba boy in Nigeria can be a unique and enriching experience. Yoruba culture is rich in tradition and is deeply rooted in the daily lives of its people. Family and community are highly valued, and children are often raised with strong values such as respect, obedience, and hard work.

One of the defining aspects of Yoruba culture is the importance of religion. The Yoruba people have a strong belief in the power of the divine and the spirits of their ancestors. This is reflected in the frequent religious ceremonies and rituals that take place in the community. As a young boy, you may have been exposed to these customs and learned about the significance of various gods and goddesses.

Another important aspect of growing up as a Yoruba boy is the emphasis on education. The Yoruba people place a high value on learning and many families will go to great lengths to ensure their children receive a good education. This may have meant a lot of time spent studying and attending school, but it also instills discipline and a sense of responsibility.

Additionally, being a Yoruba boy in Nigeria means growing up with a diverse group of people. Nigeria is a country with over 250 ethnic groups and languages, and as a Yoruba boy, you would have had the opportunity to interact with and learn about different cultures and traditions.

Religion plays a central role in Yoruba culture. The Yoruba people have a strong belief in the power of the divine and the spirits of their ancestors. They worship a pantheon of deities, each with their own specific roles and responsibilities. Many ceremonies and rituals are conducted to honor these deities, and they are an important aspect of daily life.

The Yoruba people also place a strong emphasis on education. Families will often go to great lengths to ensure that their children receive a good education, and many Yoruba individuals have gone on to become successful professionals and leaders in various fields.

Arts and crafts are also an important aspect of Yoruba culture. The Yoruba are known for their intricate and colorful textiles, as well as their woodcarvings and metalwork. These crafts are often used in religious ceremonies and are also seen as valuable works of art.

Family and community are highly valued in Yoruba culture. The extended family is considered the basic unit of society, and there is a strong sense of mutual support and responsibility among members. This is reflected in the many communal activities and events that take place in Yoruba communities.

Overall, Yoruba culture is a diverse and rich tradition that has played a significant role in shaping the history and society of Nigeria. It is known for its deep spirituality, strong sense of community, and emphasis on education, arts and family. Also growing up as a Yoruba boy in Nigeria can be a rewarding experience that shapes you into a well-rounded individual with a strong sense of tradition, culture, and community.

CHAPTER 01

A soft Down coverlet and one thousand thread count sheets wrapped around the caramel slender sleeping body of the young woman holding her captive to her dreams. It was a welcomed cocoon of fantasy and pleasure. There he was, tall, dark, Nigerian, and handsome, the epitome of every woman's dream wrapped in a bow just for her. They had been friends for most of her life, and now that she'd graduated from college, perhaps they could be much more. In the dream, they walked along the beach and watched the big orange ball in the sky fade away into oblivion. Her hand in his and his arm around her narrow waist suggested that they were lovers. No man had ever touched her in that way before, but in her dream, it was as real as her breathing. Just as he turned her head to kiss her, she heard her name being called, reluctantly pulling her from the arms of her ololufe.

"Arabinrin mi, wake up." Victoria's voice grew louder. "We've got an early flight. You knew that when you were binging The Real Housewives of Atlanta on Netflix last night. Now get up!"

Zara threw a full-sized pillow at Victoria barely missing her head.

"You are not the boss of me," Zara replied. "If you remember correctly, you are MY Oloori, and you must do everything I command you to do."

Victoria responded by grabbing another pillow and swiftly throwing it right back at her as the princess ducks under the covers.

"Get up lazy one," Victoria continued encouraging her. "Your prince is anxious to see you. He's been blowing up my phone all morning." Zara pushed back the covers.

"He has?" Zara asked blushing and beaming with delight. "He's just a friend, Victoria. You know that. He's known me since I was a babe. We are just friends!"

"Yes, that's what you think," Victoria explained. "But Sarki is hoping for much more. I can see why he's infatuated. Who in the world wakes up in the morning looking like they just walked off of a fashion runway with no makeup on but you. He came to your graduation, didn't he?"

"That's because Father made him come. He had no other choice."

"Sarki didn't want to have another choice. I've told you since we were teens that he's in love with you, but you like to pretend that's not true."

"He's never said anything to me about dating."

"That's because he knows your father would kill him if he did. Speaking of your father, what lame reason did your father give for not coming this time?"

"Victoria," Zara cautioned, "you are talking about your king."

"Yes, and he's also your father," Victoria continued. "He should have been here yesterday for your graduation. You graduated at the top of your class, and you have made our people proud. Why can't he see that?"

"He's busy."

"He's always busy," Victoria said before a momentary pause. "Zara, you make time for the people you love. He's never made time for you."

"He loves me, Victoria. He just doesn't know how to show it. Running a kingdom is a full-time job."

"No, Zara. I am sorry to say this," Victoria said with sympathetically. "He does not love you, but I do," she said reaching out to hug her friend.

Zara pushed her away.

"You don't understand the ways of the kingdom," Zara replied before turning away.

She knew Victoria meant well, but she was blinded by her affection.

"I have been your best friend since we were in grade school. I can count the number of times on one hand that he has been there for you," Victoria insisted. "You spend all your time doing what he wants, but he never gives you anything in return."

"I thought we were here to have fun," Zara said turning back around to face her friend. "I've waited twenty-one years for this day. You promised me a good time, and this doesn't feel like fun."

Zara, that's called deflection!

The two of them stood staring at each other in awkward silence.

"Listen, let's talk about this later," Zara suggested. "In the meantime, let's agree to disagree. So what time are we supposed to meet Sarki? You know he hates to wait for anything."

Zara walked to her closet, pulled out a pair of blue jeans and a burgundy striped polo shirt, and asked, "Do you think this is fitting for a queen on a girl's trip?"

"You would look ravishing in my grandmother's mumu," Victoria laughed. "Me, on the other hand, I would have to have a whole glam team on call."

"Look girl," Zara said, "I don't have any ugly friends. And if I remember correctly, you had half the boys in the palace compound in love with you by the age of eleven. Men are fascinated by brains and beauty, and you have both in abundance, especially after you put on a little lipstick."

"Why thank you, Arabinrin mi," Victoria smiled. "You are a very wise royal."

Her feet dancing while sitting Zara exclaims, "It's time to party! Let the weekend begin. The queen has spoken."

"Not quite yet, my precious. You aren't rocking that crown just yet."

"You always have to have the last word. Don't you?"

"Yes, your highness," Victoria said as she curtsied her way into her bathroom.

With both women in their respective bathrooms in the master suite, the showers were running, flatirons singing, and a hip-hop chorus filled the air. Suitcases stuffed to capacity with clothes, shoes, and makeup were thrown on the bed. Once the job was done, two very beautiful women were on the way to the time of their lives. At least they thought they were.

The black Range Rover was idling while Sarki waited for the ladies. He deliberately came a half hour later than scheduled because it was their habit to be late. But today they were breaking their own record. The valet approached him about the wait, and he explained his dilemma. What the guy didn't know was that he would have waited to the end of time if it meant he would spend it with Zara.

He had great affection for his baby omo arakunrin, but she was not his future iyawo. Zara was his key to the throne. He was madly in love with her and the idea that he could be king someday. Now that she had come of age, he could properly court her, with the king's permission of course. He had worked on gaining the king's favor since the day he returned to the compound from college. He had made his way up the ranks as a security expert. He was now the head of that department.

He was the first son of a local equestrian, and his father was convinced when he was born that he would someday be royalty. The family's bloodline was rumored to be linked to the throne, but this was a tale that had been fabricated in the huts of their ancestors based on an illicit rendezvous with a local woman who was thought to be a paramour of the king.

It wasn't that his father was delusional; he was simply a man who was convinced with every fiber of his being that his son deserved to be on the throne. His passion was infectious, and Sarki bore the conviction of his baba in his very soul.

He would have accomplished his goal sooner, but the king was adamant in protecting Zara. He went through great lengths to provide the highest level of security for her. Even the king did not have access to the princess twenty-four hours a day, seven days a week. He began cultivating their relationship when he was training her for combat. The king required her to go through all of the rite of passage activities that the boys in the kingdom experienced at the age of twelve. He was shocked by her willingness to learn. She often surpassed his expectations. Then when she was eighteen years old, she spent a summer at the Amari Training Camp for women warriors; she graduated with flying colors.

With such a strong masculine influence in her life, it was a wonder that she was the gentle soul that she was. There had been absolutely no compromise to her virtue or love relationships in her life. Here we were in the 21st Century, and the king still required his daughter to be a virgin until marriage.

In Sarki's mind, all of this worked to his advantage. She would be mere putty in his hands once they were engaged. They would start trying to get pregnant early in the marriage. He would definitely win the king's heart by giving him his first male grandchild. This would solidify his position as a royal, and he could someday sit on the throne as ruler over all of the Dala Dynasty.

That's why this weekend was so important. He was finally in a position to charm the princess, and he had plans to win her heart. His very future depended on it. He had been training for this role all of his life, and he would not fail.

Zara called the hotel lobby for the concierge to send up a bellman for their luggage. The *Live at Chelsea Festival* was in London, and they were told that it would be at least thirty minutes before they could send someone. Both women sat down in the luxurious living room with an extra cup of coffee discussing their plans for the day. Breakfast at the airport was fast becoming brunch, and the women knew Sarki was probably tearing up the lobby's Veranda carpet in anticipation of their arrival.

"Que sera sera," Zara thought contently. "Whatever will be will be."

She was tempted to call room service; they both were ravenous. They ate early in the evening, but that was over thirteen hours ago. Victoria offered to share her Snickers candy bar that she found at the bottom of her purse, but Zara refused because it was suspect of an earlier assault. That woman could always find food somewhere, whether they were in the bush or in a cosmopolitan city like Brussels. She had seen her at her best and at her worse. They were true friends, and they had been for over two decades. Matter of fact, she was her only friend. Just as she was reaching for her cell phone, it rang. Victoria was convinced that it was Sarki, but it wasn't him. It was the king.

Oba Jaiye never called unless it was of the utmost importance for the kingdom. Zara's whole life had been based thus far on a series of events that required her attention as a royal. Her father had sent her away to boarding school as soon as she was able to walk, and then there was college. She wanted to attend a coed campus after spending most of her academic life with the female gender. Her father again sent her to another institution that was for women only. He said it was for her protection and that royals had to make sacrifices because the kingdom came before anything. He felt because she'd had no mother to mentor her that she needed the guidance that could only be provided in an environment that fostered the advancement of young women without the distraction of the opposite sex. She had not agreed with his logic, but he was the king, and she was his daughter. Zara was raised under the premise that her father always knows what best.

She didn't know what else to do because her father was right about one thing; she's lived a sheltered life out of necessity. Compared to some of her peers who now had several children or a successful career, she had accomplished nothing worthwhile except the diploma that now laid at the bottom of her suitcase. She had to get a grip on her life, she was no longer a child. Some kind of way, she needed to relay that to her father. He was relentless in the control and manipulation of her life, but it was now time to show him that the mango had not fallen very far from the mango tree. She would prevail for once in her life. Shaken by this sudden bravado, she answered the phone.

"E Nle o, Baba," Zara said sweetly. "I pray you are well. How can I be of service to the kingdom today?"

Zara's father had always been an enigma to her. He was an excellent provider. He made sure she had an excellent education both inside the compound and outside, and he gave her every new technological gift imaginable. Wasn't that love? She had gone back into her bedroom to take the call for the sake of privacy. Victoria had supersonic ears that could hear a pin drop. She was known to maximize the volume when the person was near and dear to her heart.

Oba Jaiye gave her a directive that required immediate acquiescence: "*Come home immediately.*"

He was expecting American dignitaries to visit the palace. Her presence was required. Soon after, the phone went dead. There was a knock on the suite door, and she heard Victoria talking with someone. The girl's trip weekend was off. She immediately regretted having to tell Victoria. She took one last look at her cell, shaking her head. She closed it and went into the living room. Victoria was sitting in a burgundy armchair glaring at an envelope with a Dala Dynasty palace seal.

"That was your father, wasn't it?" Victoria asked.

"Yes."

"The weekend?"

"I must go home to the palace immediately to handle some kingdom business," Zara said sadly. "I'm sorry."

"I should have known that he would ruin everything," Victoria sarcastically replied. "Sarki is going to be pissed. He's been waiting all this time downstairs in the restaurant."

"He probably already knows that our trip is canceled. He's usually on my security team texts."

"That explains why his texts stopped."

"Look, I'll make it up to you..."

"This is going to cost you a lot more than a dinner at a five-star restaurant or a spa day," Victoria warned. "I just graduated from college, and I'm finally free to be the woman I want to be.

Zara felt so bad anytime she disappointed her best friend.

"It was my hope that we could cross this coming-of-age precipice together," Victoria continued. "But when the kingdom calls, you must go."

Zara let out a sigh of relief. She was so grateful to have such an understanding friend. "So, what is it going to cost me?" Zara asked.

"I am going on a trip to Nairobi, and you are going to pay for it."

"Done!"

"You know I love you, don't you?"

"Yes. That's why you're not paying for a shopping trip in Paris."

Zara and Sarki made their way through the private airport to the king's plane. A shiny brand-new silver Embraer Lineage bearing the purple and gold Dala Dynasty palace emblem awaited them on the runway. It was a perfect day for flying. Blue skies with puffy white clouds that looked like popcorn greeted them as they embarked on the air stair. The wind suddenly picked up to welcome them. She playfully teased Sarki when his hat blew off and he had to run the distance of the runway to retrieve it. Zara smiled. At least they would be on the plane together for six hours.

Upon their entering the plane six men immediately assumed the position of attention with remarkable precision. Sarki shouted, "At ease." They adopted a parade rest position, but remained standing until Zara was sitting.

An older gentleman with slightly gray hair and a chest full of medals stepped forward to greet her: "E Kabo, Your Highness."

"Kaabo, Vincent." Zara replied cordially. "I see my father has acquired a new toy."

"Yes, Your Highness, and it has all the modern bells and whistles for a premium flight fit for a princess."

"Well, this will be more than a flight home I suspect. Can I anticipate an adventure, Vincent?"

"Absolutely, Your Highness."

Vincent had been on her security team since she was a baby. He was one of the few men that her father trusted with her life. He had earned every one of the medals he proudly wore on his chest in scrimmages with neighboring tribes, and he even once stopped an assassination attempt on Oba Jaiye's life. After that, he was reassigned as a palace guard. He was offered the position of the king's security chief, but refused because he'd fallen in love with a certain dimpled princess with luminous eyes and a chubby face. Vincent never missed a chance to regale her with this story and many others about her youth. He seemed to instinctually know when she needed a fatherly touch and would freely comply. But the years apart during her academic training had made these encounters few and far between. Now that she was considerably older, her position required a totally different decorum.

Sarki, on the other hand, was much younger than Vincent and more ambitious. He wooed her father with his astute military acumen and easily won his respect. Oba Jaiye had a distinct talent for identifying the best of the best and used that skill to build a military regime that rivaled that of any of the larger countries on the continent. Sarki had been a key to the successful recruitment of military experts from all over the world to fortify the Dala Dynasty. Quiet as it was kept, that's why the kingdom was at peace, and the king could quickly avenge a wrong. He had the fighting power behind him to back up his military arrogance.

Zara wanted Sarki to sit beside her, but to her disappointment, he was in the set of seats across from her. Vincent was her flight companion, and even though they had a lot of catching up to do, her ravenous imagination would have preferred the handsome head of security to be closer to her so that they could recoup some of the time this unexpected summons had taken from their weekend adventure. She should have known that he wouldn't want his men to know about his amorous intentions for her. He was truly loyal to the kingdom through and through. It was obvious that he was disappointed when he came to the room to pick her up and wished Victoria safe travels. But he quickly recovered, and it became royal business as usual. Especially when the limousine showed up to take them to the private plane.

She attempted to start a conversation when they were in the car, but her father kept Sarki on the cell phone with kingdom business until they arrived at the airport. She would have to think of another way to get his attention. Perhaps on the trip from the airport to the palace, she could steal an opportunity to see what was really in his heart. Could he actually be in love with her? Victoria would swear it was so, but she'd never been in love before, and no other man had ever approached her for fear of retaliation from her father.

Love was complicated. She knew she was interested in Sarki, but was that because he was the only man in her world? He was attractive, smart, and loyal, but he hadn't won her heart just yet. She was curious, but not enough to defy her father or her position, so he would have to make his intentions known. But she could put herself in a better position to be on the receiving end. Until then she would have to concentrate on the kingdom matters at hand to keep her mind occupied.

Zara turned her mind to the protocols, policies, and programs that would fill her calendar the minute she stepped off the plane. In the absence of a queen, her father relied on her to fulfill that role in addition to her other duties. Actually, college had been much easier than her responsibilities at the palace. She picked up her cell phone and called her palace secretary giving her instructions to meet her first thing in the morning and inquired about the Americans that would be visiting soon. She had not heard anything from the king's assistant except to be prepared for a level one dignitary, which meant the entire palace compound would be in a tizzy until everything was perfect for their guests. Zara smiled.

Her father was probably wielding every royal power move he had to get this done in such a short span of time. He was in his element, which meant he was happy. She would have to be satisfied with the disruption of her plans, especially if it brought her closer to him. He was not at her graduation ceremony, but she would make sure he noticed the woman that she'd become in the span of the year that they were separated.

She could have gone home for the holidays, but Zara wanted her father to miss her enough to ask her to come home. Hoping that her absence would draw him closer soon became apparent as the immature antics of a lonely desperate child who was trying to get her daddy's attention. When he didn't call, write, visit, or inquire about her well-being, she assumed he was terribly busy. Only Victoria knew the heartbreak that she had experienced.

Well, he has called now, and she couldn't wait to see him. Regardless of his putting the kingdom before her, he was still her baba, and right now he needed her. At least that's what she tried to convince herself of for the rest of the airplane ride home. Zara closed her eyes and laid her head back on the pillowed headrest of her seat. She needed a pleasant escape, and since she couldn't have it with the real thing across the aisle, she chose to seek him out in her dream world. As the raging ball of fire sat down on the horizon, he took her in his arms and gently caressed her lips with the sweetest kiss that she had ever known.

Chirping turtle doves welcomed the convoy of black Range Rovers that carried the most precious cargo of the Dala Dynasty, the princess Zara. She was always amazed at the sense of peace that followed her return to the palace. In the world she was always performing, excelling in her academics and extra-curricular activities. That had been her job, but this was her purpose. Living the life of a royal was all she knew. Others may have been dissatisfied with a life like hers with all of its protocols and structure, but she was extremely grateful for the opportunity to serve her people, her kingdom, and its king. She sighed.

"Zara, are you okay?" Sarki asked.

"Yes," she answered. "Just enjoying the familiarity of our motherland. It's good to be home."

Sarki inquired because he knew he would need to give a full account to the king once they arrived. They now sat side by side in the back seat. It had literally taken an act of God to get Vincent to sit up front with the driver. She finally persuaded him by feigning the need for an important conversation with the head of security before they arrived at the compound. It was looking like all of her effort to be alone with Sarki was fruitless. He had been on his cell the entire time they were in the car. She could only get his undivided attention for seconds between calls. A few miles down the road, it appeared that a window of opportunity was now opening.

"Princess, what is it that you wanted to discuss with me?"

"Sarki, do you always have to be so formal? I miss my old friend. Don't you remember the good times we had as children?"

"Yes, but we are no longer children. I thought you told Vincent that you needed to speak to me about something important."

"I just wanted to say I am sorry that our weekend plans were interrupted. The three of us haven't had a lot of time together over the last few years. I was looking forward to this weekend."

"No need for an apology. We both know that our kingdom responsibilities take precedence over everything else."

"Yes, but it shouldn't be that way all of the time."

"What made you say that, Zara? Sarki asked surprisingly. "Your father would be deeply offended if he heard such blasphemy. You of all people should know better."

She searched his eyes, and for a moment, she thought she saw true regret. He quickly slipped back into his security chief persona.

"It is what it is, Zara," Sarki said. "The gods have deemed it as so. We are mere chess pieces on the chess board called life. It would do you good to remember your responsibility as the daughter of one of the most powerful men in North Africa. You shouldn't take it lightly."

"Sarki, are you scolding your princess?"

"No, Your Highness, just reminding you of your duty to your country. One day you may be ruler of the Dala Dynasty, self-sacrifice will be something that you do on a regular basis."

His cellphone rang, and he was immediately immersed in another conversation about some security issue regarding the American visitors.

Zara rarely sulked, but today she denied herself the privilege of putting on a fake persona. She was not happy with Sarki. His words had cut deeper than he knew. She was well versed in her responsibility and didn't need her childhood friend to remind her of it.

Victoria must have been teasing her about his interest because here they were alone, just the two of them, and all he could talk about was palace politics. He hadn't seized the opportunity to share his heart with her. Quite the contrary, he instead used it to remind her of the very thing that she was seeking a temporary diversion from. Must she be a royal every second of the day? Why couldn't he just take a trip down memory lane with her? What would it have cost him to do something as simple as that? A few moments of his time? A smile? Perhaps Sarki wasn't who she thought he was. She'd let her heart become wrapped up in a fictitious vicious circle of lies and somehow, he never got the script.

Well even if a fraction of what Victoria had shared with her was true, he would have to work much harder to win her over. He wasn't the only one that could run hot and cold in a matter of seconds. She quietly put her royal mask back on and moved over closer to the darkened car window, hoping that no one could see the tears running down her cheeks. She wasn't angry, just disappointed. Rejection hurts.

They were ten minutes away from the palace gates, and the memory of her conversation with Sarki was firmly placed somewhere in the back of her mind. It was showtime, and she was required to step into her role with dignity. She pulled out her compact and checked her makeup and hair. Satisfied that everything was in order, she returned to her study of the landscape outside of the window. Her homeland was beautifully exotic. Even someone with a weary soul could find resurrection after experiencing its initial allure. She could easily be a candidate for its healing powers today.

The palace gates were a grand testimony to what was hidden behind their walls. This extravagant set of gates rose high and even more majestic than those at Buckingham Palace. The artistic handmade metalwork accents spoke of a genteel time in history, and the bold mechanical and electronic accessories hidden within were state-of-the-art. The gates used an array of floral, royal, and vintage symbols that spoke to the significant status of the Dala Dynasty on the continent.

There were two smaller elegantly crafted gates uniquely positioned for the viewer to enjoy. One grand gate in the center stood higher and shined more distinctly than the rest. This gate personified royalty. It was a sharp contrast to those designed for practicality and protection in the villages.

As the sleek black automobiles filed one by one through the gates, Zara remembered who she was and why she was here at this very moment. It was time to cast aside the silly dreams that she had allowed to plague her restless nights. The man sitting beside her could no longer be the romantic lead on the stage of her mind. He wasn't as interested in her as she thought... or was it the simple callousness of his position that controlled the dictates of his heart? What did she know of love anyway?

Her position relegated her to a life of isolation and loneliness. Was that to be her fate forever? She sure hoped not. But for now, she must bid the memories of her old childhood friend, Sarki goodbye. It was too hard to determine if he was a friend or foe now that he'd become a man with a kingdom mission. It hurt to do so, but it had to be done. As he so expertly put it, they were no longer children, and she had responsibilities to the throne.

She was in the next to the last vehicle in the caravan. From her viewpoint, she could see the entire palace staff awaiting their arrival in the glorious colors of their native land with the biggest smiles she had seen in a long time on the faces of people who looked like her.

Vincent turned around and looked at her before saying, "Welcome home, Princess Zara. Your kingdom awaits."

"Yes, aburo. It does."

CHAPTER 02

Houston heat was a savage beast in mid-July. Everyone on the construction site was drenched wet from sweat and humidity. Add the fact that they were over budget and understaffed made the insufferable heat another reason for the popping vein protruding from the construction foreman's neck. The other was he had to tell his men that they wouldn't get paid for another week again. The last time he lost half of his work crew. This time he'd be surprised if any of them stayed. It's one thing for day workers to quit; it's another when his entire management staff walks off the job. Ezra hadn't been on a worksite as a construction foreman in a long time. Here he was in a metallic box called an office sweating like a pig before Christmas dinner because the air conditioner wasn't working trying to save his company.

Desperate times called for desperate measures. Ezra Johnson had been forced to leave his cushy downtown office to prove that he was still in the game to win it. At first his men thought it was some kind of *Undercover Boss* power play. It amused them that the CEO was rolling up his Gucci sleeves and getting down dirty with them in the field. But these men weren't fools. He'd been there for over a month. Most of them had been working construction long enough to know when to cut their losses and run before the whole thing went bust. It was evident that he was headed that way.

It was merely a matter of time before his other Texas sites got the message that E. Johnson Construction & Son was near bankruptcy. He only had a few days before it became common knowledge in the industry that he had overpromised and under-delivered on his last two government contracts. The signs were there that the company was in trouble two years ago. Now anyone worth their salt in this business could see that too. The competition was like vultures circling its prey just waiting for the news to hit the streets that his doors had closed, permanently.

In its day, E. Johnson Construction was always a step ahead of the rest as a premium provider of engineering and construction services. At one time the company provided jobs for over 25,000 employees and had an estimated yearly revenue of over 11.6 billion dollars. A nasty divorce, the pandemic, and the recession changed all of that.

Ezra had done all he could to salvage what was left of his dignity and his company, but times were hard. He imagined himself up for the challenge. He wasn't a quitter. Lesser men would have either left the country or jumped out the window of a really tall building. They sure had plenty of those in Texas.

This project had been his last hope. If this crew left after his announcement today, he would be forced to hire illegals and convicts. The list of compromises was getting longer and longer. At one time he'd been a man of great faith. Now he couldn't even bring himself to say an *Amen* because of the disappointment he had in his God. Where was he when you needed him? His forefathers were missionaries; some of them died for their beliefs on the mission field. It looked like he too was going to die on his. *The Lord giveth and the Lord taketh away.*

He grabbed a cold bottle of water from the fridge just as the phone rang.

"Hello," he answered.

"Mr. Johnson?" Manuel, his assistant said.

"Yes."

"There's a lady out here who wants to speak with you. She says that she's the chairman of the board for the company. Do you want me to bring her up to your office?"

Ezra's leaned back in his chair exasperated.

"Sure, Manuel. Bring her up."

Ezra attempted to straighten up the trailer before his dignified guest arrived. He could hear the tapping of her heels on the makeshift concrete walkway. Then there was a rapid knock on the door. He opened it to what should have been his salvation. The grin on her face told him that she was a bearer of bad news. The former Mrs. Ezra Johnson Sr. was the acting chairmen of the board, a title she'd won in their divorce. She now owned fifty-one percent of the company, and it was payback time for their irreconcilable differences.

"*It is better to live in a corner of the housetop than in a house shared with a quarrelsome wife,*" came to mind as Ezra stepped aside to allow his ex-wife's entry.

Suzette Johnson offered Ezra the only ultimatum available, relinquish all managerial control to her, and she would supply the necessary cash and manpower to restore it to its previous glory. He had twenty-four hours to respond to her offer, or the board would ask for his resignation within the next forty-eight hours and take his company away from him. They offered him a mere twenty-five million dollars severance to go away and never come back. She laid the papers on his desk, did a graceful pivot, and walked out of his life again. This time his one true love was in her hands. She knew it and relished every second of his pain.

Soon after she left, Ezra decided that he needed a day off. He released his crew and decided that since the ship called his company was already sinking, a boat ride might be in order before it was repossessed. He did his best thinking while out on the water, and Galveston seemed the ideal place for some of that. Most of the men were so happy to get away from the sweltering heat that there were few inquiries about pay. So, he could put that on the back burner. He was sure a day or two on The *Missionary Maiden* would ease his mind.

Soaring down I-45 heading toward Galveston with the top down on his red Mercedes-Benz SL, Ezra began reminiscing about his past and contemplating his future. He'd stepped away from the family business of saving souls to build a company that would finance charitable initiatives that were Christ-centered. His father actually started the first construction company to help build churches, schools, and homes for the indigenous people in third world countries. He was quite successful in getting the financial backing that he needed because of his family's reputation in the ministry.

When his father passed and left him the business, he decided to take it to the next level. The success of the business became his mission field. Unfortunately, he'd left God out of his business plan. He honestly couldn't say he didn't know better because he did. In some kind of way, he was a prodigal. He still believed, but his pursuit of money had consumed him.

Suzette was wife number two in less than ten years. If he was honest with himself, he didn't love either of them, not like they deserved. Then there was the disappointment of a son by his first wife, Julia, who ran off with her personal trainer. Ezra Jr. was as spoiled as they came. His mother made sure of that. Most of his life, he'd been an egotistical brat who detested him as a father because he "wasn't around to raise him." Ezra Sr. had his regrets, but the boy had now become a man, and he just graduated to bigger toys and a larger expense account.

The company was his mistress and now, well, she was about to leave him too. He had exhausted all of his resources. There wasn't a bank in Texas that would loan him another cent. He was done. What was a man to do when he was at the end of his rope?

He hadn't been in the building-for-God business for long. Ezra couldn't remember exactly when he made the transition, but he knew that was a major turning point in his life. He'd left the pathway that God had for him a long time ago, he was sure of that. He still believed, but he hadn't seen the inside of a church since two years ago when Suzette was trying to get him to go for marriage counseling. That didn't last long. Then there was the divorce, and now he was busy trying to salvage what was left of his company. He felt justified in concentrating all of his energies on building the business. Didn't God help those who helped themselves? Wasn't it the American way of doing business? If nothing else he was victim of a failed system. Regardless of who was to blame, he had twenty-four hours to come up with a solution. He needed a miracle, and he needed it NOW!

The murky bay waters caressed the ship's bow in anticipation of a brief voyage. The breeze was a nice alternative to the stuffy trailer office that he used on the construction site. There were few places in Texas that he could now call *home sweet home*, the Galveston Bay was one of them. *The Missionary Maiden* welcomed him with open arms. She was one of the few women that he could say still appreciated his attention. The day the divorce was finalized, he found himself at an Aviara boat sales lot and instantly fell in love with a navy AV40. She was his refuge and sanctuary when the metal and the concrete got to be too much.

Ezra lifted the anchor and readied the boat for a brief voyage and some much-needed quiet time on the water. When he returned back to shore, he had to have a solution for his money problems or be prepared to retire early. He didn't like it, but those were his only two alternatives. His gut instinct told him to pray. But he hadn't talked to God in a long time. He just wasn't sure God would answer him. But desperate times required desperate measures. Ezra fell to his knees on the floor of the boat and said three words that immediately changed his downward trajectory: "Help me God."

God smiled.

He awakened several hours later in that same spot to the lull of the lake swooshing up against the hull. He looked at his watch and realized he'd been there for five hours. His back was telling him to get up and relocate to the luscious queen size bed in the cabin below, but his arthritic knees were slow to respond. He managed to sit down and lean against one of the bar stools. Well, bourbon was out of the question. He didn't think he could reach the bar after being on the floor that long so he just sat there trying to find a happy memory to cloud out the pain in his knees and of the day. Had he ever been happy? In his fifties, he had woman problems, forties, he was taking the company public, thirties, he was building his company, in his twenties, he was getting equipped to run his company and trying to pacify a demanding wife.

Sure, there been happy moments, but no extended seasons of happiness except when he was a boy. Yes, he was happy when he and his father went to Africa that summer to build houses. He remembered living in a palace and having access to everything a boy could imagine. That was nice. But what was really special was his relationship with Oba Jaiye. It was the first time he had anything resembling a sibling in his life, and as the summer progressed, their friendship blossomed into true brotherhood.

His last contact with the prince was the weekend before they both went off to college. The king flew him in as a graduation present for his son. The monarch was in ill health, and his son needed a distraction. By now Oba Jaiye was probably king and busy with the affairs of running his kingdom. But... what if he reached out to Oba Jaiye. Perhaps he could help provide a temporary solution to all this chaos. It was worth a try.

"It's 2:30 am here," Ezra thought. "That means it should be about 8:30 am there."

He reached in his pocket, pulled out his iPhone, dialed the palace number, and asked to speak to the king. After a brief pause that seemed like hours the rich baritone voice of his boyhood friend filled the air.

"Hello, my American ore atijo," Oba Jaiye's voice boomed across the phone.

"Oba Jaiye," Ezra smiled. "It's so good to hear your voice old friend."

The sun was shining unusually bright through the windows of the corporate boardroom on what should have been a dismal day. After thirty years of pouring his all into this company, Ezra was about to lose it all.

Suzette called an emergency board meeting for noon that day to start the takeover proceedings, and everyone was in attendance except Ezra. Some came out of curiosity, others because they were people of integrity, and they had the best interest of the company in mind. Unfortunately, Ezra had no allies in the room to champion his cause. Suzette had spent months courting the key board members and ultimately convinced them that she was their best option.

The meeting was called to order. Suzette gave a status report on all of the company's holdings. Just as she was about to make a motion for Ezra's termination, three unexpected guests showed up. Two strong armed African men dressed in black with dark sunshades and a meticulously dressed blonde who knew her way around a boardroom entered the room. Melanie Bragg of Bragg Law PC and her African escorts carried two titanium briefcases. Ezra chose Ms. Bragg because she was one of the few friends and business associates that would still return his calls, and she owed him. She was also sassy, articulate, looked stunning in a designer suit and would easily upstage a prima-donna like Suzette. Add the charm of a southern belle on a hot day in Texas, and you definitely had a winning performance. Surprised by the unexpected visitors, Suzette tried to regain control of the room.

"This is a private meeting," Suzette said sternly. "Please leave, or we will have security escort you from the building."

"Is this not the emergency board meeting for E. Johnson Construction?" Melanie asked.

"Yes. But you weren't invited."

"Excuse my manners," Melanie said. "My name is Melanie Bragg, and I represent Mr. Ezra Johnson, the CEO of this company and Oba Jaiye Akinyemi of the Dala Dynasty."

"Ezra, I know," Suzette said. "But who is Oba Jaiye Akinyemi?"

"King Akinyemi is the primary stock holder in this company as of ten o'clock this morning."

The whole room gasped in surprise.

"According to this document you gave Mr. Johnson yesterday at noon, as a managing partner, he is to either make a matching $50 million-dollar deposit in E. Johnson Construction corporate accounts to keep the company viable, or resign. Well, he has sent me here today to ask you a question."

Melanie motioned to the African men, and they placed the briefcases on the table. She nodded, and they opened the latches and flipped open the lids.

"Will a billion dollars do?" Melanie asked.

Ezra and Oba Jaiye stayed on the telephone for several hours discussing their past and future. He hadn't laughed like this in a long time. Once he shared his dilemma with the king and the proposition to bring restitution for his help once the company was back on its feet, it was a done deal. In a mere matter of hours everything changed. The king was not only magnanimous in his assistance but also with his resources. Even Ezra was surprised at how swift his upside down world had been turned right-side up, just because he made a telephone call in the middle of the night on a lonely boat in the heart of the Galveston Bay. As he was about to sing the praises of his dear friend, a stark remembrance of an earlier call hit him... God had heard his prayer and answered it.

Morning came quickly. The seagulls beckoned him for their breakfast and because of his quick getaway he'd forgotten to bring food for the voyage. This meant that he would need to go back to shore sometime soon. He rustled his graying beard and thought about what was going on in the company boardroom about right now. Oba Jaiye had advised him to take a few days off before returning to his managerial role at the company. The board needed time to regroup, and his ex-wife needed time to lick her proverbial feathers.

He chuckled. Suzette was going to be pissed. This just might send her back to Betty Ford. Welcome to the big leagues baby. You win some and lose some. Their vicious divorce had totally annihilated any feelings he had for her, but he didn't wish her ill will. Even though she'd set the stage for his demise both professionally and personally, he just wanted to be rid of her meddling in his company. Well now, by the grace of God, he'd gotten a reprieve.

The next step was to reach out to his wayward son. He hadn't heard from him in a couple of years. When it was evident that he was going to lose another wife, he ran. He did get a text from him last week when his American Express was confiscated. He wired him what little discretionary funds he had. Ezra got no reply back.

Ezra Jr. was born at the wrong time in Ezra Sr.'s life. He was building his company and had a demanding wife. He soon found out after marrying Julia that *pretty is wasn't the same as pretty does*. They hadn't planned for a child so early in their marriage, but it was obvious after the honeymoon that they'd both made a horrible mistake. His religious upbringing wouldn't allow him to divorce her, so he tolerated her temper tantrums for fifteen years because of the kid. It was a relief when she ran off with her ex-NFL player personal trainer. His first divorce was easy. She had filed for it to marry her new boyfriend. Now they live in The Heights in a remolded home with four little mixed kids that all look like her current husband. The jury is still out as to whether that's a good thing.

His son came to live with him for a brief period of time after their divorce. He was seventeen. One day after dinner he asked how much money he planned on leaving him. He gave him an estimate based on his personal wealth at the time. He asked if he could have it right then. He'd come up with a plan for emancipation from both of his parents and laid the details out in a PowerPoint. His son told him that his mother had already signed the papers, shared a copy, and requested an answer by close of business the following Friday. His final words were: "You owe me for not being the father I needed. Pay up, and I'll disappear out of your life forever if that's what you want."

Got to give it to the kid—he'd done well investing in some successful dotcoms the first four years. But then he turned twenty-one, the magical age of consent and lost any semblance of common sense. Women, drugs, and partying were his poison. He never made it to college. According to the local tabloids, there was a different woman on his arm every week. Always blonde with blue or hazel eyes, tall and slender with a Miss America figure, just like his mother.

She'd called once to stage an intervention, but by then the company was in deep financial trouble, and Ezra couldn't get away. He sent an Amex Platinum card instead that was tied to his personal account with a note that said, "Here's $10,000 for treatment. That's the best I can do right now."

Their relationship had become purely transactional. He regretted it, but those were the cards life had dealt both of them. He was a rotten father, and Ezra was a rotten son.

Oba Jaiye had discussed a plan that may give them both a second chance. He loved his son even if he had a bad way of showing it. It grieved his heart that he wasn't the father to him that his had been.

Memories of those African summers and the many missionary trips where he worked alongside his Dad came flooding back. They were a team on the mission field until his last dying breath. They were working in the Sahara Desert the summer of his nineteenth birthday when his father got malaria. They were thousands of miles from a hospital, and his father was too sick to move. They realized during the night that it would be a miracle for him to live until morning. He did, but he never got well enough to make the trip for medical attention. Ezra was crushed. With his last breath, his father prayed an Abrahamic blessing over his life.

He remembered the words just like it was yesterday:

> *May God give you all the blessings with which He blessed Adam, Enoch, Noah, Shem, and Abraham. Everything that He said to me and everything that He promised to give me and your forefathers, may He attach to you and your descendants until eternity—like the days of heaven above the earth. In Jesus' name, Amen.*

When had he left God and why? But he would deal with that hot topic later. There were more pressing matters at hand. He would need another miracle to bring his son onboard because Ezra could be as stubborn as he was.

Crazy Alan's Swamp Shack was one of Ezra's favorite restaurants at Kemah. He would walk a mile for their Catfish and Shrimp Feast. He'd put in a call to his assistant, and she'd taken her sweet time getting back to him. Right when he was about to feast on a succulent piece of catfish the telephone rang.

"Hello."

"Mr. Johnson, you called?" A female voice asked.

"Yes, Rachel. Where have you been? I called over an hour ago."

"Mr. Johnson, did you forget that you fired me last week?"

"I did?" Ezra said. "Well, you're re-hired. I need you to send the company helicopter to the Mediterranean to pick up my son."

"Mr. Johnson, I would love to come back, but you haven't paid me for over a month."

"How much do I owe you?"

"Four thousand dollars," Rachel said. A pause indicated her hesitation. "Are you still the CEO of the company?" She asked.

"Last time I checked I was."

"Okay... If that's the case, can you Zelle me the money because I really need it."

"What's Zelle?"

"You have it. Just go to your bank. They'll show you how to send it."

"Can I use my cell phone?"

"Yes, but..."

"Just walk me through it. I'll send it right now."

"Okay. Go to the Trust Bank app on your telephone. Your username and password should automatically come up."

"It did."

"Add me as a contact."

"How do I do that?"

"Just type in my name and telephone number and save it."

"Done. Now what?"

"Put in the amount and click send."

"Done. Did you get it?"

"OMG! Mr. Johnson did you mean to send me $10,000?"

"Yes. I did. You're back on the clock, aren't you?"

"Yes sir. Thank you so much!"

"No. Thank you! Now about that helicopter, here's the location of the yacht my son is on. They have a helipad, so it shouldn't be a problem. Have a car pick him up and bring him to the marina, boat slip number twenty-seven. I'll be waiting."

"What do I tell the pilot to tell your son?"

"Tell him that there is a family emergency that requires his immediate attention."

"Okay, Mr. Johnson. When should I report back to work?"

"Monday. Come to the worksite and dress accordingly. That's going to be your temporary home until we can get this project on target again. Understand?"

"Yes sir."

"Text me when my son arrives."

"Yes sir."

"I need to go now, or a perfectly good meal will go to waste," Ezra added. "Have a great day!"

"You too, Mr. Johnson. Bye!"

Rachel was a true trooper. She'd been his assistant for the last fifteen years, but he had to fire her because he could no longer pay her. She was just that loyal. He went back to his meal with the utmost confidence that he would see his son later in the day.

Two buxom blondes crisscrossed the king size bed, one facing the bottom and the other the top. Ezra Jr. was in the middle of this tangled mess. The swishing sound of helicopter blades woke him up. His vision was blurred, but the cabin was an utter disaster. The remnants of last night's party were strewn all over the room. Bras, panties, evening dresses, his underwear, and an empty bottle of Moet Chandon was upside down in a sparkling discarded pump that had seen better days. Just as he refocused on his visual target, there was a loud knock on the door. Sounded like the border patrol. He knocked one of the moaning women on the floor as he sat straight up in the bed to check for Big C.

"E., man wake up," a male voice yelled from the other side of the door. "There's a helicopter out here waiting for you. Your old man sent it. Something about an emergency."

"Is he dead?"

"How would I know, man?"

Ezra Jr. pushed the other woman off of his legs, put his pants on, grabbed his wrinkled shirt and a cigarette.

"He's going to wish he was if this isn't important," Ezra Jr. muttered as he left.

The Missionary Maiden was being readied for another voyage. This time father and son would be its crew. Ezra couldn't remember when he'd spent a full day with his son, nonetheless a whole weekend. It was going to be a challenge, but strangely he felt up to it now that the business was in good hands. Oba Jaiye's men had taken over the management of the worksite, giving him a brief respite. The crew not only got their pay, but they also received a few days of paid vacation.

Rachel texted him that Ezra Jr. had arrived and was on his way to the marina. He'd brought a couple of steaks, some potatoes, and a few other necessities that they would need for their weekend trip. He'd even brought Ezra some clothes for the trip. Look at him, being a father. It's better late than never.

But Ezra Jr., or E. as he called himself now a days, was a grown man with his own desires and opinions, so Ezra Sr. was going to have to handle this situation in a man-to-man-manner. When Oba Jaiye first proposed that they abide by the blood covenant they'd made when they were boys, he thought the idea was ludicrous until he realized it was another way to justify his actions. Arranged marriages were not a thing of the past, but not as prevalent as in his great grandfather's day.

Oba Jaiye's daughter needed a husband, and he needed to save his company. The bride price was half of his kingdom. He was worth twenty-five billion dollars. At first, he found it strange that the king had not selected someone for the dynasty, but when he explained that he felt it was best to bring someone from the outside so that he could train them to be the ruler he wanted them to be, it made his intent clearer. He had not guaranteed that he could convince his son to marry Oba Jaiye's daughter. But if he could make it happen, it was the difference between a billion-dollar loan and a 12.5-billion-dollar gift.

Ezra had taken great care to explain the current degenerate status of his son. Oba Jaiye was even more convinced that their plan would work. It took a while to convince Ezra that his son was not in a bargaining position because he was broke, busted, and disgusted. He had no future, no money, and no hope. A relationship with his daughter could bring him all of that and more. Now, it was almost showtime. He had faced titans in his industry head on before. But this was different. It was his own flesh and blood.

The limousine pulled up to the dock, and out of the back seat crawled his son. Tall like his grandfather, blonde like his mother, and a mirror image of his father. There was no denying this one. He stumbled to the boat, obviously on the tail end of a high. It pained him to see what his son had become. He knew his father would have been sorely disappointed in him, not Ezra Jr. For a moment shame filled him, but as instantly as it tried to overcome him, it left.

"Old man, you ain't dead yet? The son greeted his father as he tried to maneuver the gangplank.

He stumbled and fell toward his father, who caught his son before he toppled off the plank. But his son indignantly pulled away.

"Let me go old man!" The son slurred. "I can't believe you ain't dead yet. I need the rest of my inherit… Why don't you just dieeeeeeeee." In the blink of an eye, Ezra pushed his son in the water.

"What the… You pushed me in the water," a dripping wet E. shouted.

"I thought you needed a bath," his father replied. "You sure smell like you do. I'll meet you inside when you get some manners. Remember I am your father, whether I was a good one or not."

"You mean sperm donor, don't you?"

"Whatever. You're here, aren't you? Stay in the water and catch pneumonia for all I care." Ezra turned toward the boat.

"You're going to leave me out here?"

"Yep."

"Come back, Pops," E. began to plea. "I'm drowning out here."

"You ready to show me some respect?"

"Yes sir."

"Good."

Ezra extended his hand toward E. Surprisingly, E. tried to pull his father into the water with him, but Ezra jerked him onto the boat with a swift jerk.

"Playtime's over," Ezra said. "Get your but into the shower and into some dry clothes. They're on the bed in your cabin below."

"Yes sir," E. replied as he slinked off to his cabin.

Ezra set sail for deeper waters once he was sure that E. was in the shower. It was already apparent that it was going to be a long weekend. But for once his son was his priority, at least for the next week.

It was mid-afternoon before E. returned to the deck. He didn't look much better than he did when he arrived, but he was clean.

"You been in the gym, old man?" E. asked. "Wait a minute, where are we? Did you kidnap me?"

"No. You're not a kid anymore. Shut up, sit down, and eat," Ezra replied as he pushed a plate toward his son.

For a minute, E. glared at his Dad then sat down and tore into the food like a ravenous lion.

"Eat much lately? Ezra taunted.

"Why'd you send for me?" E. asked. "I got some business back on the yacht that can't wait."

"You mean Brittany and Dee Dee?"

"How'd you know about them? You're still having me followed, aren't you?"

"I promised your Mom I would keep an eye on you."

"You keeping your promises to Mom now?"

"I've always kept my promises to her. The timing has just always been off between us. But we're not here to talk about that. We're here to talk about you."

"Why the sudden interest?"

"I have a proposition for you."

"I don't want to work at the construction company. I never have, and I never will. So, turn the boat around and take me back to Houston."

"Okay. I'll do that. It seems that you aren't open to new possibilities. I just hope the next time I see you, it isn't in a casket. Have a good life son," Ezra said before getting up from his chair to turn the boat around to go back to the shore.

"Where you going?"

"Taking you back where I found you."

"You're not going to fight me?"

"No."

"What kind of father are you?"

"I guess you'll never know. This was your opportunity to be fathered, but you said no."

"I'm almost thirty."

"Yes, and from the looks of it you need some help. You're an addict, a womanizer, and broke. When you came to me at seventeen, you convinced me that you had a better plan for your life. I reluctantly supported your independence. Twelve years later, you are a complete failure. I'm offering you a chance to become the man that you were destined to be. Because you are a grown man now you have to make the choice. From the looks of it, it's a life and death decision for you. When you are ready to talk, let me know. Should I turn the boat around?"

"No. I'll stay the night."

"Good. See you in the morning."

After he heard E. snoring, Ezra decided that prayer was his only option. He fell to his knees for the second time on this life-changing voyage. But this go round, it was for his son.

The smell of coffee percolating and bacon frying pulled E. from his bed. He found his way to the galley where his Dad was in his bare feet and shorts humming some religious song.

"Good morning, Son."

E. nodded. "What's for breakfast?"

"Eggs, bacon, and toast. Coffee's over there."

Ezra put a plate in front of his son.

"You should have been a chef," E. said.

"No. Construction is my thing. For me, there's nothing like seeing what's on a blueprint come to life."

"So, is this thing you want to talk to me about construction related?"

"No. It's about marrying an African princess."

"What???" E. spit out his coffee. Wiping his chin, he said, "Did I hear you right?"

"Yes. Do you remember when I told you about how your grandfather and I use to go on our missionary trips to North Africa? Well, one summer I met a young prince. We became blood brothers. I mean literally. We even drew up a contract that listed the parameters of our agreement. I haven't returned since your grandfather's death. But that boy is now a king, and when the company was going bankrupt, he was there for me."

"So, what does this have to do with me?"

"Part of our covenant agreement was that our firstborn children would marry."

"How old were you when you made this agreement?"

"We were ten."

"So that's over thirty years ago, and you want me to be a part of this sham of an agreement?"

"No. I don't. It's got to be your choice."

"So, you say he gave you money to save the company. That's why my Amex Card didn't work. You sold me to him for your company?"

"No. If you don't agree, I will have a huge loan to pay off, and be obliged to my friend for the rest of my life. Before the pandemic we were on track to make our first billion. I estimate that we will have the loan paid in full in ten years. But where will you be in ten years?"

"How much did you get from your blood brother?"

"A billion."

E. whistled. "How much of that is mine?"

"Spoken like a true cocaine addict."

"Look, Pops I just do the Big C socially. I don't have to have it."

"Is that why you were rummaging in my bar and the medicine cabinet last night?"

"Don't change the subject. Are you telling me that you didn't promise your friend the king that I would marry his daughter for the loan?"

"No. It was actually his idea."

"He must not think much of his daughter, or he doesn't know me."

"He knows about you. He did a thorough investigation before he made the offer."

"So, what's in it for me?"

"A chance for a better life and the opportunity to do something good in the world."

"What does she look like?"

"What do you care? She could be three hundred pounds and missing her two front teeth. You need a change."

"She wouldn't happen to be blond, would she?"

"No, I don't think so, but she comes with 12.5 billion dollars. Part of that is her dowry."

"Whew!!!"

Ezra started to clean up the kitchen. "We'll be headed back in thirty. Get ready."

"Wait, Pop. What are the terms of this agreement?"

"You sure you want to know?"

"Yeah."

"You've got to get clean, live in Africa, and stay married to the princess for the rest of your life."

"Have children and all of that kind of stuff?"

"Yes."

"You mean I can't divorce her, ever?"

"No."

"I'd have to be faithful like a regular husband and help her raise our children?"

"Yes."

"Pops, I don't know. Forever is a pretty long time."

"Again, it's your choice."

"So, who gets the money?"

"It's placed in a trust until the marriage is consummated, and then part of it goes to your parents and the other to you."

"How much?"

"Those terms aren't determined until the king approves you as a husband for his daughter."

"So, you are saying that I must go to Africa, win the heart of a black woman that I don't know, and charm her Dad who is a king into letting me marry her?"

"Not exactly, but that's close enough."

"So, would Mom benefit from this arrangement or just your company?"

"Your mother would get half of the dowry, whatever that is."

"Does she know about this?"

"No. This must stay between you and me. I don't want to get her hopes up."

E. dropped his head. "She's had a hard time with me, hasn't she?"

"Son, all I know is she's happy now, and I want her to stay that way. If you have an opportunity to contribute to her happiness, I think you should take it."

"Pops..."

"That's all I have to say about it. What do you want to do?"

"Can I think about it a while longer?"

"Sure."

"Okay."

E. went to his cabin. His father decided to go fishing. In the quiet of the afternoon, Ezra continued to pray as he thought about their earlier conversation. He was surprised E. still had a soft spot for his Mom. That gave him hope that he wasn't as far gone as he thought he was. Maybe, just maybe the boy would say *yes*. That would put a whole different spin on what happened on the boat this weekend. He knew that he couldn't let his son go back to the life he was living or he'd lose him for good. He'd lost two wives, and E. was his only child. He was tired of losing people. He'd lost his Mom at an early age and then his Dad before he was really ready to let him go. He was capable of love, but there was always that fear that he would lose those most precious to him. Today was the day he had to totally surrender that fear to God. It was the only way he could do what was necessary to save his son.

Daybreak came swiftly. E. was still sleeping, and Ezra was preparing to return to shore. They'd been drifting for about a day and a half with no real destination in mind. Frankly, he didn't know what his son would decide to do, but he would support him either way. He felt a bizarre peace this morning, something he hadn't felt in a long time. There was a settling in his soul. Instinctually, he knew that everything was going to be alright. He decided to get some additional fishing in while he waited for his son and his decision. Just as he was unhooking a speckled trout, his son suddenly appeared.

"Pops, I think I'm going to be sick," E. said before he upchucked last night's dinner over the side of the boat. His father handed him a paper towel and went to get him some seltzer water from the bar.

"Here drink this."

E. gulped it down. After swiping his mouth with the back of his hand he said, "I've made my decision."

"Really?"

"Yes. I will go to Africa, just as long as you are going with me."

"Okay. Straight talk from this point on. Agreed?"

E. nodded his head.

"Well, we need to deal with your addiction."

"Yeah. I guess we'll be going back to shore today. You going to send me to one of those fancy rehab centers?"

"No. We're actually going to do it out here."

"What?"

"You've been to those fancy rehab centers before. Have they worked?"

"No, but this time is different. I've got a reason to get clean."

"Yes, son you do. And this time we're going to do something different. I'm going to help you. Me, you, a Telehealth doctor and God can do anything."

Sheepishly E. asks, "Are you sure Pops?"

"Absolutely. You're here aren't you?"

It was a long five days on *The Missionary Maiden* now turned hospital. E. had already started the withdrawal process. The sleeping and fatigue were evident the first day he was on the yacht. Then there was the vomiting, sleep deprivation, loss of concentration and motor control. The third day was the worse. Ezra literally had to pick his son up in his arms out of a urine-soaked bed and shower him. That was the day that E. begged his father to take him back to Houston to his mother. Ezra proposed a compromise, getting his Mom on the telephone. E. eventually refused because he didn't want her to see him in that state. Later that night, the hallucinations and tremors started, and he wept most of the night while Ezra held him in his arms. A worn out and exhausted father fell into bed the next morning around 6:00 am. At noon, he was awakened by his son standing at the door of his cabin calling his name requesting something to eat.

He hadn't cared for his son like this since the boy was a toddler with the flu. His mother refused to care for their son when he was sick, so he was the home team medical professional anytime the kid got ill. Falling into this role as caregiver for his adult son was a comfortable place, but that didn't mean it didn't break his heart every time he heard him scream out in the night for help.

On the fifth day, E. was much better. He was able to keep his food down, and his overall appearance pretty much returned to a semblance of normality. They sat on the deck listening to the waves caress the hull when E. asked his father when they were returning home. While inquiring of his readiness to do so, his father turned to deliberately face him. They locked eyes for a few seconds, and both men really saw each other for the first time in a long season of misunderstandings. It was in that moment that they both knew that better days were ahead of them. Two days later, they turned *The Missionary Maiden* around and headed home.

It soon became obvious that his son was serious about going to Africa. His whole demeanor changed when he talked about this new adventure. Ezra just hoped it was enough for him to make a permanent change in his life. E. teased his Dad about the downfalls of arranging a marriage without seeing his prospective bride. His father joked about the raw deal that the princess was getting in a husband. They laughed a lot that day on their way back. It was encouraging to see his son in great spirits.

As the boat approached the slip, a welcoming party of one stood on the dock. The glimmering sun framed a tall statuesque maiden with golden hair and a figure that unbelievably disguised the fact that she was a mother of five. E. looked at his father to gain his approval. After a brief nod, he jumped onto the dock and captured his mother in his arms. She laid her head against his chest and wept, but not before she whispered a silent *thank you* to her ex-husband.

E. Johnson Construction was up and running at full speed. The board had unanimously voted to rescind the request for Ezra's resignation and reestablished him as managing partner. Rachel got a promotion to lead forewoman on the government job in Houston in her boss 'absence and ran the site better than any man that had come before her. It didn't hurt that the armed security men from Africa were now assigned to her and also possessed business management skills in the area of building and engineering construction. On the Monday following the boardroom upset, a group of lawyers headed by Melanie Bragg and a group of state auditors ascended on the company and requested an audit of the company's books. Suzette indiscriminately left the building in a huff assigning her Vice President of Accounting to handle everything. It was rumored that she got on the next flight to New York City for some rest and relaxation until the dust settled.

Ezra and his son pulled up at his condo and retired for the night. E. thought it was a good idea to stay with his father until he had completed the detoxing process. Ezra agreed but reiterated that he wasn't under house arrest. He could go and come as he pleased. His mother and her tribe made frequent visits to Ezra's home. She proclaimed his miraculous transformation to anyone who would listen to her.

The only problem he had with his father was his missing cellphone. He'd searched everywhere for it and even put the locator on to try to find it, but it was nowhere to be found. They both finally came to the conclusion that it had gotten lost in the lake when he fell in. Once upon a time that cellphone was his lifeline. It was remarkable that after his time on the boat, it was no longer as important as he thought it was.

Father and son returned to the construction worksite that next Monday. He asked his father if there was something he could do besides sit around and stare at the walls. His father gave him a good once over and assigned him to the daily work crew. E. worked like he was exorcising the demons of his past with every rock he demolished with his sledgehammer. The rough work was good for him and to him. Ezra kept a close eye on his son during this critical transition in his life, and his son clung to him for the moral support that he needed to leave his past behind. They had a lot of catching up to do, and Ezra was grateful that God had given him a second chance to be a father to his son.

Both men counted the days until they would be on their way to the Dala Dynasty. One man was excited to see his old childhood friend again and the other a little apprehensive to begin his adventure.

CHAPTER 03

Dala Dynasty was in an uproar in anticipation of its esteemed guests. Zara got caught up in the festive momentum. Mesmerized by the romanticism of being home, she was wrapped up in reliving the joys of her childhood. It was a form of escapism for her.

The reality of her rarely seeing her father was evident. She told herself that it was okay because everyone was busy, especially Oba Jaiye. Yet, she had been gone a whole year without as much as a telephone call from him until the day after graduation. Eventually, she told herself that it was something she had absolutely no control over, and she would have to make the best of an awkward situation.

There was plenty for a princess to do in the palace compound and even more outside of its walls. Zara called her press secretary to her office, and they began to set up a seven-day tour of the dynasty. She met with her team of advisors to further identify the problem areas in the dynasty that hadn't been addressed in a while. She would be back just in time for the festivities.

North Africa was famously known for its beautiful mosques, booming markets, and ancient ruins and panoramas, but the people were its true jewel. Zara made a point to celebrate them as often as possible. The world thought of North Africa as a place of poverty and inward turmoil, but there had been peace in Dala Dynasty for over one hundred years. The people were agricultural and entrepreneurial in nature. A hard day's work in the kingdom was worn like a badge of honor. The people worked hard and played hard. The palace was known to host a celebration for an entire month drawing in its inhabitants from all over the dynasty for the exquisite lodging, cuisine, entertainment, and athletic games.

The princess was a kingdom celebrity because of her generosity and kindness. News of her impending arrival passed quickly throughout the dynasty, and the people started to prepare for her arrival. She was scheduled to start in the northeastern part of the kingdom. Her security team, headed by Vincent, awaited her in the wee hours of the morning for an early departure. Zara looked back at the palace with mixed emotions. She was enthusiastic about her journey but saddened that her father had not joined the farewell party. *Que sera sera* had become her permanent mantra. She entered the Range Rover with a determination that she would not let anything of no importance influence her right now.

Zara was in for a long trip, but it gave her an opportunity to take a hard look at her future. Would being a royal ever be enough for her? She was still discovering who she was as a woman. The majority of the women her age in the kingdom had two or three children by now and settled into some form of relationship, be it marriage—either polygamous, monogamous, or a consensual union.

Her father wouldn't stand for anything other than a monogamous marriage with a member of the opposite sex as dictated by the Holy Scriptures. She laughed as the realization of her current status as an old maid hit her hard. It wasn't because there hadn't been suitors, but they all had to meet her father's approval, which none of them had secured.

Sarki had been a possibility for a while, but her infatuation had grown thin, and she realized that their relationship was based on their proximity versus a genuine admiration for each other. She'd expected him to be on this tour, but her father had him assigned elsewhere. Vincent was a pleasant replacement. He regaled her with stories of her childhood and her late mother throughout the duration of the trip to their first destination. He specifically made a point to share with her how her father and mother met and the love that they shared in the early days. He made her heart smile with his warmth and fatherlike attention. She had no need to worry about anything, so she didn't.

They had scheduled seven days on the road to seven villages. The first one was to a village that needed a school. The construction would begin after the groundbreaking ceremony. The palace provided all the materials. Men of the village had been commissioned to build the school by their chief. Zara would present the materials and a special ebun for the chief. She was honored with flowers from the children and an elaborate kaba from the women of the village. It was the beginning of several successful goodwill efforts on the part of the palace, at least that's what Vincent told the king to sell him on letting Zara go on the tour.

She had no knowledge that the king had originally said "no." Vincent had sensed her restlessness, and she ended up on tour, and he ended up with a week's vacation from his palace duties. It was a win-win situation for everyone. Little did Vincent know, the king had acquiesced because he did not want Zara to get wind of his plans for her, the plans that would totally revolutionize her life.

The second stop was at an orphanage that needed water wells to be built and their pantry restocked for the winter months. Here, Zara was mesmerized by an abandoned infant with AIDS. She sat for most of the day cradling the baby girl in her arms and caring for her like she was her own child. Before she left, she hired a private nanny to care for the child and made her promise that she would write her weekly about the baby's progress and send pictures. Through the dark tinted windows of the Range Rover, no one could see the princess as she wept when she left the orphanage, except Vincent, and he spent the remainder of the day praying that God would quickly mend her broken heart.

On the third day of the tour, she arrived in a more sophisticated city where the day was full of magazine interviews and television appearances. Totally worn out by evening, she had room service deliver her dinner to her hotel suite. Zara fell asleep soon after, and Vincent had the remains of her dinner tucked away in the suite's kitchen.

They left early in the morning for the fourth city on the trip. It was in a rural agricultural town where Zara met with the local chief for a tour of his crops and the new farm equipment that they acquired. She spent her evening at a reception hosted in her honor where all the farmers and their families gathered to showcase the products that they sold all over the continent of Africa. At this event, she read a special accommodation sent from the king praising the chief for his excellence in product delivery and his efforts to modernize their agricultural pursuits. They received a monetary gift for their innovation that was well received by all.

On the fifth day, after a long ride, the princess and her entourage landed in a huge metropolitan city where she was scheduled to be the featured guest at a museum opening. Zara spent most of her day relaxing in her suite until her glam team arrived. When she stepped out of her suite into the limousine, it was apparent that she was the queen of the ball. She danced until the early morning hours after giving a speech to a standing-room-only crowd of supporters.

On the sixth day, she was back in the rural part of the dynasty visiting a military hospital laughing and joking with the soldiers, sharing stories about her escapades at an all-girls school, and eating lunch with the medical staff. She presented the hospital director with a sizable check to add a new infectious disease wing to the hospital.

On the last day of her journey, she went to a meeting on a reserve managed by The Sahara Conservation Fund. She and the managing team discussed how the king could best support their efforts to improve the conservation of various local species from extinction. The visit also included a tour of the reserve and a photo opportunity. This particular meeting only lasted until midday, freeing Zara to get some anticipated rest before returning home.

Just as she was fluffing up her pillow, the telephone rang. It was Victoria. She knew then that her evening plans were shot. They were on the cellphone talking about Victoria's arrival, what she was wearing, how her hair would be styled, how many eligible bachelors of the who's who would be at the festivities, and rescheduling their girl's trip until she dragged a weary body into the Land Rover the next morning.

Between Vincent and her personal assistant, she was kept abreast of what was happening at the palace. Her father still hadn't briefed her on her responsibilities at the celebration. She was actually too tired to contemplate his reasons, so she pushed her seat back in the reclining position and went to sleep. Not before Vincent put a blanket over her saying, "Sweet dreams my dear princess." This was a game they had played since her childhood. It was usually accompanied by a bedtime story, but she was too big for that. She returned his sentiment with a nod and a smile.

They arrived back at the palace closer to midnight. She was whisked into the west wing of the palace, which housed her quarters and those of her support staff. As expected, her itinerary for the week of festivities was on her home office desk. There was a battle between her curiosity and her eyelids. Sleep won, and she was off to bed after assuring Vincent that she would be fine for the festivities that started the following night. He, of course, was concerned that if she did not meet the approval of the king at this event, he would lose favor with him.

Little did Zara know, the American guests had arrived, and at this very moment her father and his old childhood friend were sharing a bottle of Redemption 36-Year-Old Bourbon, reminiscing about old times, and solidifying the covenant arrangement that would join their two families together forever.

"Oba Jaiye, you have become the man I always knew you would be," Ezra Sr said raising his glass. "I am so proud of you."

"Well, thank you, my Ore mi," Oba Jaiye replied. "I believe we both have done well. In business there are ebbs and flows like there are in the Kano River, but it doesn't stop the river from performing its main purpose of providing refreshment and nourishment to those who depend on it. You are that river. That's why I believe your son is going to be a fine addition to our family. He comes from good seed. Your father was an awesome man of God. And you, well, you have surpassed him in the construction business as it should be. Ezra Jr. can't help but become a great prince because of his lineage."

"Talking about my son, now that you've seen him, you are positively sure he is the man that you want to marry your daughter?"

"Absolutely!"

"Why?"

"Because of our blood covenant for one. I don't make it a habit of breaking my agreements, especially with the people I love. We have history. I am as committed to our arrangement as I was the day we climbed that hill when we both were ten and full of mischief. So, let's move forward. We shall have many grandchildren together." The king chuckled and took another sip of his whiskey.

"What about your daughter? What if she doesn't agree to this arrangement?"

"She will."

"What makes you so certain?"

"She knows her responsibility to the kingdom. It will always be a priority in her life. I raised her that way."

"I see," Ezra said. "Do you have a picture of her?" He asked looking around the room. "I don't see any."

"No. That's part of the surprise. Hopefully, it's love at first sight for both of you."

The two men chuckled and took another drink. Soon after the evening came to an end. Ezra wanted to check in on his son before he called it a night. E. was actually sitting cross-legged on his bed with his computer on his lap.

"Son, I just dropped by to say goodnight. If you are busy, I can check in on you in the morning."

"No, Pops, come in. I was just checking the Internet for pictures of Princess Zara. The only pictures I can find are those of her when she was a young child. I wonder why is that?"

"Oba Jaiye said it contributes to the element of surprise about tomorrow night's festivities."

"He doesn't want me to see her before then?"

"No."

"Now, I'm really worried about her being three hundred pounds and missing her two front teeth."

"Don't be. Remember, you haven't signed the betrothal contract yet, and you don't have to. We can get on the same plane that brought us here and go home tomorrow if you want."

"No, Pops, I want to see this thing through. Besides don't you want to spend some time with the king?"

"Of course, but your happiness is very important to me, and your mother is already going to have a fit when she finds out what we are up too."

"Don't worry about Mom. I can handle her."

"You sure?"

"Yes."

"Okay. I am having Melanie review the contract, and she's scheduled to meet with us early in the morning, so I need to call it a night."

"Okay, Pops. Can I ask a favor?"

"Yes, son."

"Can we pray?" E. said. "If Mom knew what was going, on I'd be asking her, but since this is whole thing is one big secret, I guess you're it."

"Sure son, but I'm positive your Mom is a lot better at it than me."

"I heard you praying on the boat."

"You did?"

"Yes."

"That's odd, you never said anything about it before. Son, those were just the ramblings of an old man trying to touch the heart of a heavenly Father who had also been in a similar predicament."

"I see, well it took me a while to figure some things out about you. I'm sure you can understand that."

"Of course," Ezra said as he sat down on the bed beside E. and held his hands saying, "Let's pray then."

As he went into prayer about the outcome of tomorrow's events, he specifically asked for wisdom for his son and that most importantly God's will be done in both of their lives as they embarked on this new adventure.

There was a constant flow of traffic in the palace. Oba Jaiye made an appearance greeting both men at breakfast and sitting down to enjoy the meal with them. He apologized for not being available to take them on a tour of the palace. He needed to ensure that the preparation for the evening's festivities were competently handled. He also explained that he had kingdom business to take care of. Dignitaries were coming in from all over the continent, and he personally greeted every one of them as a gesture of goodwill. Ezra encouraged him to continue with his planned schedule for the day. He assured him that they were fine and would see him at tonight's event.

Oba Jaiye took this opportunity to ask E. if he had any questions about tonight's protocol. He assured the king that the assistant he had assigned him had done an excellent job of preparing him. The king also asked him if he had any questions about his daughter. E. looked directly at Oba Jaiye before he spoke. His curiosity had gotten the best of him. He requested that the king describe her physical attributes. Ezra Sr. noticed that the king's eyes became murky with what appeared to be regret. No, it wasn't regret; it was actually pain. The verbal response then came quickly, like a knife being withdrawn from a sheath in the heat of battle: "She is as delicate and exquisite as her late mother."

As rapidly as this window to the soul of the king opened, it closed. E. started to apologize, but his father stopped him. Oba Jaiye excused himself quickly from the room, but not without promising to be available at a moment's notice if they had any questions. Both men locked eyes. Something wasn't right with the king. Ezra had his suspicions, but only time would tell if they were valid.

The Zoom notification rang for their morning meeting with Melanie. She was on the other end in Houston preparing to share a synopsis of the betrothal contract that Oba Jaiye had drawn up by his legal counsel.

"E., this contract is a legally binding contract that requires you to commit to marry Princess Zara one year and a day from today. On your wedding day, Princess Zara will receive the monetary value of half of her father's kingdom. As her husband, you are entitled to 25% of any monetary award that she receives.

"During that year you must court the princess in her home in Africa. The west wing of the palace, where I assume you are staying now, will be your home for the duration of the betrothal period. You can opt to stay in Lagos, but all expenses would then be your responsibility. If you choose to stay in the palace, you will receive a monthly stipend of $10,000, and all of your living expenses will be taken care of by the government of Dala Dynasty. You will be provided a manservant and male secretary to assist you. By living expenses, I mean food, clothing, shelter, transportation, and medical costs. You will be given a weekly agenda that will include physical and combat training, cultural sensitivity training, and etiquette training. You will also be required to escort Princess Zara on goodwill tours, to social and political events hosted by the dynasty, and spend a large portion of your time in the dynasty courting her.

"It is of the utmost importance that Princess Zara remains a virgin during this time period, and you must agree to not violate her in any way during the courtship," Melanie managed to say before snickering. "You must also agree to a weekly drug test. Any questions?"

"No," E. said. "You did a great job of breaking it down in layman's terms, Melanie."

Ezra Sr. asked, "What is the termination clause?"

"There isn't one. It's expected that if your son signs the contract that he and Princess Zara will marry."

"Son, would you like to add one?"

"No."

"You know you can still change your mind."

"Pops, I told you already that I want to see where this leads."

Ignoring his son, he asks Melanie, "What do you recommend, Melanie?"

"I can't answer for Ezra Jr. Only he can do that," Melanie said. "Honestly, I wouldn't do it, but considering what you have to gain, E., it might work for you. You have to personally weigh the pros and cons." She paused. "I can say this; if for some reason you terminate the contract, you may be responsible for any monetary investment that was made in or for you during the duration of the betrothal. Do you think your son would be in danger Ezra if he changes his mind?" She asked.

"No. But it could get very uncomfortable for him if he does," Ezra replied.

"I see," Melanie said nodding. "It looks like they are going to great lengths to be fair and equitable by making this arranged marriage very profitable for you, E. I must ask, are you doing it for the money?"

"Honestly, at first I was," E. said slowly. "But now, well... I've never completed anything in the thirty years I've been on this earth, and I want to see what the man I am becoming is capable of."

"What if the marriage is a loveless one?" Melanie asked.

He chuckled. "Then it will be even more of an adventure. I've never had much difficulty in convincing a woman to do anything. I welcome the challenge."

"Won't you miss your family?"

"I've been a coke fiend for the last two years," E. admitted. "I didn't even know they existed most of that time. I will definitely see them a lot more than when I was caught up in that life. Didn't my father tell you about where he found me?"

"No, he didn't," Melanie said turning her attention to his father. "Ezra?"

"Another time, another place," Ezra said with finality.

"Will I at least get an invitation to the wedding?" Melanie asked.

"I will fly you here personally," Ezra said. "Thanks, Melanie. Make sure you send the bill to Rachel."

"What bill? The king already paid it. It seems that he's going out of his way to show his goodwill in regard to this arrangement. Have you seen her yet E.?"

"Nope."

"Not even a picture?"

"No, but it wasn't because I didn't try."

"Well, have fun, you two, I've got an early appointment in the morning, and my bed is calling my name."

"Ezra?"

"Yes?"

"Be safe out there in the jungle."

"You know, Melanie, this has actually always been a place of refuge and peace for me."

E. interjected, "Then why are you so concerned about me?"

"Because you're the only son I've got, that's why!"

Princess Zara was awakened by the theme song from the sitcom *Girlfriends*; it was her comedic ringtone for Victoria. Sleep was a precious commodity before a major event because her palace duties often required her to greet guests well into the wee hours of the morning. She fumbled for the phone, reluctantly supplying a grumbled salutation. She was not a morning person by any means. Today she'd planned on sleeping until midday, but Victoria had ruined those plans with her early morning call.

"Wake up, Zara," Victoria sang over the phone. "Any civilized princess would be up by now making sure everything was in order for tonight's festivities."

"That's not my job yet," Zara said gruffly. "What do you want? I need my beauty sleep. You know father loves to have his hand in the middle of everything when we have palace events."

"Well Miss Grumpy, I have an updated list of the eligible bachelors that will be in attendance at the gala," Victoria said with glee. "I couldn't wait to share the juicy details with you. So, forgive me for interrupting your precious beauty sleep. Now, the latest additions are the tall dark brothers from the southern kingdoms that are known for their million-dollar smiles. Girl, you know they are all fine like Idris Eba. I am so glad that you are my bestie because the gala will be a single girl's haven for fun."

"Don't worry, Zara. I'm sure the king has ensured that there will be plenty of potential suitors for you, girlfriend. They'll all be hoping to get next to you and that dowry. Everyone who's anybody will be there except for my cousin. Poor Sarki, he is not happy that the king sent him to America on business."

"Really?" Zara questioned. "Did he say what Father sent him there for this time?"

"Girl, you know how he is about all this *NCIS* and *Criminal Minds* stuff. He's not going to share anything with anybody about his 'mission.' I think sometimes he's too loyal to the king. Speaking of the king and his kingdom, I hear that the ambassador from Kenya is bringing his son. I checked him out on the Insta. Girl, he is a delicious chocolate drop with hazel eyes. He reminds me of Michael B. Jordan. I wonder if he's looking for a replacement for Lori Harvey? I hear..."

Zara drifted back into dreamland while Victoria spilled gossip about the who's who in the dynasty. Eventually, she hit stage R and started snoring.

"Zara, Zara wake up girl!" Victoria yelled. "You actually fell asleep on me? Well, I am not going to repeat a word I said. You'll have to find out on your own. Have you seen the Americans yet?"

"What? No."

"Why not, Zara? Does your father have you locked up over there or something?"

"Remember, I just got back last night, and I'll spend the entire afternoon getting ready for this evening's festivities. Why do you have to be the last person I talk to in the evening and the first person in the morning?"

"Because I'm your best friend, and that's what we do, even if one of us is a sleepy princess. I hear the American ambassador is also attending the gala tonight."

"Really? Interesting. I guess Father invited him to make the Americans feel more at home. I'd better check the protocol for this evening's event."

"How can you be so nonchalant about everything? It seems everyone in the kingdom is excited but you."

"Victoria, you have to remember that this is work for me. My father expects me to be available to cater to whatever inclination he has in addition to being hospitable to our guests. Add that to a seven-day tour of the dynasty. I am exhausted."

"Well, I better let you get your rest then *Princess*. I don't want your Daddy mad at me because you have bags underneath your eyes."

"Vickie, I'm sorry."

"I understand, but you better be prepared to have some fun this evening because I'm going to make sure you do."

"Alright."

"Sweet dreams, Princess."

"Thanks for understanding. You are a jewel. Bye."

"Bye."

Zara laid back on her royal pillow and closed her eyes. Her maidservant collected the telephone from her sleeping hand two minutes later. The princess was out for the count.

The king stepped away from his busy schedule with the intent to check on his daughter. He dismissed his security detail and sought the solitude of his bedroom. Locating a small remote in the back of one of the top drawers of his stately mahogany dresser, he aimed it at the bookcase in the rear of the large room. The bookcase swung open like a very large bank safe door and exposed a hidden room. It was filled with computer monitors and security camera feeds. These were really the eyes of his kingdom. The king entered the room and sat down in the only computer chair available.

There she was fast asleep on her antique gold and leather upholstered queen size bed. Its magnanimous size engulfed her small frame. He envisioned young Ezra fitting nicely beside her in it. What a pair the two of them will make. He was articulate, charming, tall, and handsome. Oba Jaiye was a great judge of human character, and that young man was full of potential.

He wondered what she would think of his surprise. It didn't really matter, but he was still curious. He'd been extremely meticulous in planning out every detail of her betrothal. After all, she was the only heir to his throne, and he needed her to marry someone he could control.

When his childhood friend called him, he knew it was an answer from the gods of his forefathers. He'd been looking for a satisfactory suitor, but every one of his prospects had fallen short. Sarki had come to mind, but he was more valuable as head of his security team than as a potential husband for Zara.

He was forced to come to the conclusion that he would have to create one, and Ezra's son was the perfect candidate for the position because he was in desperate need of redemption. Tonight, he would give an academy award performance as the doting father, and his kingdom would love him even more for it.

Taking one last look at Zara peacefully sleeping as if she didn't have a care in the world, he whispered to her, "Rest up, dear daughter; you are going to need it. Tonight, you are in for the shock of your life."

The palace gates were now closed. This gala was an invitation-only event. All the guests were instructed to be seated thirty minutes before the festivities actually began. The American guests, the ambassador, and other dignitaries were seated at the head table, which was the length of a football field. Ezra was placed on the king's right hand, and E. was placed beside his father. He was anxious, and it was obvious. But his father was the rock that gave him the strength to remain seated.

The parade of dignitaries began promptly at the top of the hour. The local chiefs from all over the dynasty started the royal procession. Each village represented was proceeded by a royal banner that signified its place in the dynasty. Following the village leadership were the palace dignitaries and the heads of states. Princess Zara and Oba Jaiye were the last members of the royal family to enter the room.

The princess was dressed in a silk burgundy gown with gold accents that accented her womanly curves and was complemented with an exquisite solid filigree gold crown. She was breathtaking. Her long braids were stylishly coiffured to frame her mahogany face and bring attention to her luminous brown eyes. Her makeup was impeccable. She would have rivaled any top model featured in an international magazine. This female masterpiece was an untouched magnificent jewel, a blossoming flower.

Zara was stunned to see her father at the door when she was summoned to the festivities. She expected Vincent to be her escort, but there he was in all of his royal splendor, dressed in a black Kiton tuxedo with a matching cummerbund and bow tie in the royal dynasty colors of purple and gold. His crown was gold with emerald cut diamonds accessing the diadem. Black Gucci shoes finished off his dashing ensemble. He was the type of man that made the suit shine, not the other way around. She was pleasantly surprised to see him.

"Good evening, Daughter."

She gracefully bowed. "Good evening, Your Highness."

He extended his arm. "Come, we don't want to be late for the festivities."

"Yes, Father." She took his offering as a sign of his affection, and they proceeded to the ballroom.

She was mesmerized by his presence to the point of speechlessness.

His unusual kindness to her felt strange and unfamiliar. Could he be proud of her for some reason? Her recent graduation or the tour? She hesitated to ask him for fear it would disrupt this magical moment.

There was complete silence in the elevator. He only greeted her with a smile when she found the courage to look up at him. They exited the elevator, and he squeezed her hand pulling her directly in front of him.

"Remember my dear, the well-being of the kingdom is always our priority."

"Yes, Father," she said with a curtsy.

The golden doors to the ballroom were closed. Two flawlessly attired guards were in their dress military uniforms waiting on their commander's directive to open the doors. Inside, the royal anthem started to play, and the king gave a nod. The doors swung open wide, and all eyes swept to the back of the room. The host announced the arrival of the king and his daughter, and the room was filled with unanimous applause. What the inhabitants saw was a proud father escorting his daughter into a gala, but the king saw himself as a major player on the stage of life fulfilling his destiny for the good of his people and the kingdom that he loved.

Ezra looked at E. and said, "Well, she's not three hundred pounds and missing her two front teeth."

"No, Pop's. She's not," E. replied as he intently watched the princess' regal stride alongside her father. He couldn't take is eyes off of her for even a second.

The ballroom was striking, to say the least. White ostrich plums with gold accents were placed everywhere in purple vases, and the traditional fabric of the Dynasty graced every table as a runner over a pearl white tablecloth. The chairs were white with fluffy gold seat cushions that would withstand the night's excitement. Gold banners with the names of each village hung high above its section designating the tables that were elegantly laid out for its luminaries. The larger metropolitan sites in the dynasty were identified by enormous round purple and gold banner stands with the name of the city in the center. A full orchestra in the pit played a mixture of modern international tunes and traditional African music.

The head table was signified by a backlit fabric wall of ostrich feathers. Bright beautiful color explosions of purple, gold, teal, and turquoise filled the fabric backdrop that immediately caught the attention of anyone entering the room. There was a massive digital screen that would be lowered later on in the evening for a state of the dynasty address by the king. The head table sat on a mobile dais that could be turned anyway the king designated for the pleasure of his quests. Even the servers wore tuxedos with white cummerbunds and bow ties that matched the gala's theme. The all-male crew served a seven-course meal to over twelve hundred guests.

When Zara and the king reached the head table, he made a point to introduce her to his American guests before they were seated. She acknowledged them with a nod and a smile. Her father then sat her down next to his throne. Her seating arrangement was a smaller version of his larger throne that was gold with an ostrich feather patterned cloth on the back and on the seat. They were identical except for the primary colors; her throne was all white, and his was gold. White to signify her purity and gold to signify his royal rank in the kingdom. They were slightly elevated above the other head table members. The king seated his daughter first and his manservant came to assist the king.

When he sat down, the music stopped, and the hostess announced that dinner would be served after the blessing. Catholicism was the dynasty's state religion, so a catholic cardinal blessed the food before they dined. The table was full of the finest Bernardaud china and monogrammed cutlery from France. The Waterford Crystal goblets were lined with a gold filigree ring at the top specifically made for this special occasion and would be a gift to all its departing guests.

Dinner was served on solid gold platters piled high with each delicious course being more appetizing than its former culinary selection. Soon after dessert was served, the host and the hostess presented the history of the dynasty. Following their presentation, a digital clock was set to alert the attendees of how much time they had to socialize and take care of personal matters before the king took the podium.

In the interim, Zara noticed that when she went to the powder room, the American guest's son was staring at her. She politely smiled in return and continued on her journey. Victoria met her there with tons of gossip, and they giggled and laughed until both ladies were rushing to fix their makeup before returning to their chairs. They both made plans to reconnect for morning brunch in Zara's suite. They bid each other goodbye with butterfly kisses.

Zara's security escorted her to her throne, and the king's manservant escorted him to the podium. Oba Jaiye was an elegant orator. It wasn't uncommon for him to win the hearts of his audience with his wit and charm. He began his speech sharing the accomplishments of each of the villages and the cities of the dynasty. The king then covered his future plans for the kingdom followed by thundering applause. He called Princess Zara to the podium to personally give her an enthusiastic thank you for what she accomplished in the villages during her goodwill tour. A video that highlighted her journey immediately followed. Everyone was thoroughly thrilled with the accolades and the good news including Zara. She returned to her seat; her heart rejoicing over his praise.

Then to everyone's surprise the king called his American friend and his son up to the podium. He told the story about how as young boys they became the best of friends and eventually blood brothers who formed a covenant to remain loyal to each other for a lifetime. At the king's directive, his audio-visual staff showed a short documentary of pictures of the boys playing from that summer. At the end of the video, Oba Jaiye embraced Ezra Sr. He then awarded him with the honorary position of chancellor over all of the kingdom, declaring that Dala Dynasty would always be a second home to him and his descendants.

The king handed Ezra the microphone. For a moment, he reminisced about his time in the kingdom and shared a funny story about how they met and how he was eternally grateful for his new friend because he was on his way to the worst beating of his lifetime. The audience laughed as he told his story. Then, on a more serious note, he talked about how the friendship they shared helped him recover from the loss of his mother and played a huge role in the man he had become. There wasn't a dry eye in the ballroom after he spoke. The king and Ezra embraced again. Afterwards, the king called E. to come forward. He introduced E. and then called Zara to come back to the podium. She dutifully obliged her father. So, when he placed her hand in E.'s hand, she was surprised but complicit because of their large audience.

"This day, in so many ways, is a landmark day for me as a father and ruler of Dala Dynasty," Oba Jaiye said. "It is with great pleasure that I announce the betrothal of Princess Zara to Ezra Thomas Johnson Jr. May they live long and give me lots of grandchildren, preferably male." The ballroom rang from wall to wall with applause and praise.

Victoria exclaimed, "OMG," and suspiciously fainted in the arms of the deliciously handsome stranger standing beside her.

E. felt the princess go limp beside him after the announcement. He whispered in her ear, "I've got you. Do you think you can make it through this?" She nodded affirmatively, found the inner strength to straighten her stance, and put a smile on her face.

Once the applause died down the young couple was seated together. A throne, the exact duplicate of Zara's, was added to the podium and they were escorted to them. E. continued to hold her hand while they were seated because by then she was trembling. From the outside it looked as though the newly announced lovebirds were conversing, but E. was comforting her and assuring the princess that everything was going to be alright. She on the hand was mad at her body for betraying her. Yes, the news was shocking, but she was still a royal, and when the kingdom called for her to make a sacrifice, no matter how magnanimous it was, she must comply.

E. bent toward her and questioned, "You didn't know about this, did you?"

She shook her head "no."

"You don't have to go through with this," he said. "I can say I changed my mind."

She emphatically answered, "No. It's fine. I'm fine."

The king further announced that there would be a betrothal period of one year and one day from the date of the gala. He encouraged his guests to prepare to return to the palace compound on that day for a wedding that rivaled Prince Henry and Meghan's. The crowd laughed. He then called the young couple and Cardinal Francis Arinze to the podium.

E. grabbed the princess' hand and spoke gently to Zara as they made their way up the stairs. "We are now going to sign the betrothal agreement. Are you okay with that?

She nodded "yes."

They were instructed to kneel before the congregation of dignitaries.

Cardinal Arinze began the ceremony saying, "It is the dispensation of divine Providence that you are called to the holy vocation of marriage. For this reason, you present yourselves today before Christ and his Church, before his sacred minister and the devout people of God, to ratify in solemn manner the engagement bespoken between you."

After the priest's allocution, the couple joined hands and E. said, "Don't urge me to leave you or to turn back from you. Where you go, I will go. And where you stay, I will stay. Your people will be my people and your God my God."

To E.'s surprise the princess had a quick response: "As it pleases God to fulfill my kingdom purpose, I will leave my father's house and cleave to you as my husband."

The agreement was handed to Zara first. She signed it and handed it to E. with a smile. But her eyes betrayed the true turmoil that was going on inside her.

He hesitated for a second and whispered in her ear, "Are you sure?"

She planted a kiss on his cheek and whispered, "Yes."

He signed the agreement, and the cardinal blessed the union. The cardinal then placed the ends of his stole in the form of a cross over their hands. He declared them officially betrothed, and blessed the engagement ring that the king's manservant handed to the cardinal. The cardinal gave E. the ring to place on Zara's finger. He smiled at the young couple then read John 15:4-12 to end the ceremony:

> *"Remain in me, as I also remain in you. No branch can bear fruit by itself; it must remain in the vine. Neither can you bear fruit unless you remain in me.*
>
> *"I am the vine; you are the branches. If you remain in me and I in you, you will bear much fruit; apart from me you can do nothing. If you do not remain in me, you are like a branch that is thrown away and withers; such branches are picked up, thrown into the fire and burned. If you remain in me and my words remain in you, ask whatever you wish, and it will be done for you. This is to my Father's glory, that you bear much fruit, showing yourselves to be my disciples.*

"As the Father has loved me, so have I loved you. Now remain in my love. If you keep my commands, you will remain in my love, just as I have kept my Father's commands and remain in his love. I have told you this so that my joy may be in you and that your joy may be complete. My command is this: Love each other as I have loved you."

Afterwards, the king dismissed the assembly. The host and hostess bid farewell to the assembly, and the room quickly emptied to share the good news with the world. Victoria mysteriously recovered quickly and had appropriated her cell phone from its hiding place to take pictures of her best friend and her new fiancée.

The young couple was immediately surrounded with people from the head table offering congratulatory sentiments. This lasted until 3:00 am. The king retired soon after the dismissal, but Ezra stuck around to the end waiting for his son and his soon to be daughter-in-law. When the room was cleared, Ezra, E., Zara, and her security staff retired into the Royal Lounge that was designated for the family and their guests only.

Once the guards were stationed outside of the doors, the princess turned to E. and his father and said, "Welcome to Dala Dynasty."

Both men looked at each other, and E. shook his head. Ezra was the first to speak: "Your Highness, it is my pleasure to finally meet you. It appears as if you were kept in the dark about your upcoming engagement. Am I correct?"

"Yes, but I knew the day would come that my father would choose a husband for me. It is sometimes our custom to arrange marriages with other royals for the benefit of the kingdom. Obviously, my father holds you in high regard, chancellor, or he would not have made the match."

She turned to E., "Forgive my immediate response. It just caught me off guard. I consider myself fortunate to have a year to get to know you before we are married. It appears that you knew about the betrothal?"

"Yes. But that's the only thing I knew about," E. confessed. "By the way, if you were wondering, I agreed to the marriage before I saw you because of the history of our fathers."

"I see."

"Princess, you aren't in love with someone else, are you?"

"Oh no. I guess every girl has the silly notion that she will marry for love. But I knew at an early age that would be a luxury for me if it ever happened."

"So, you don't think love is possible between us?"

She shared a heartfelt smile with him. "If it comes, it would be an added benefit."

He turned to his father and asked, "What do you think?"

Ezra scratched his head, the gold medallion her father gave him dangling from his chest begging to be noticed. "Son, I believe the final outcome concerning this engagement is in the hands of the two of you. Time will tell if you are a good match, but I have a strong sense that God is up to something. I guess we will have to wait and see."

"Princess Zara…," E. began.

"Please, call me Zara."

"Zara, please excuse me. I need to call my mother before she reads about this engagement in the newspapers."

"Your mother? She doesn't know either?"

"No."

He reached in his pocket for his cell phone and remembered that everyone's cell phones were confiscated before the gala. He sheepishly grinned at the princess and asked, "You wouldn't happen to have a cell phone, would you?"

She reached into her purse, pulled out her phone, and handed it to E.

"Thanks."

He Face Timed his mother. She immediately picked it up.

"Hello, darling," his mother said once she saw his face.

"Hi, Mom."

"Why are you calling me from this number?"

"It's the princess' phone."

"The princess?"

"Yes. She's a real royal, and I have her telephone."

"Really?"

"Really."

Where are you?

Africa.

"What time is it there?"

"It's somewhere around 3:30 am."

"Goodness gracious boy, why are you calling me at this time of morning?"

"I wanted to share some good news with you."

"What's that?"

"Princess Zara and I are engaged."

"You're what? You've only been there for two days. How in the world did that happen? Put your father on the phone immediately," his mother demanded.

At that moment, Princess Zara stepped into the picture and said, "Hello, I'm Zara. It's my esteem pleasure to meet you."

His mother gasped. She took a few seconds to visibly regain her composure before saying, "She's beautiful, E."

"Yes, she is Mother."

"It's nice to meet you, Princess Zara."

"Likewise," Zara said smiling. "I can't wait to meet you in person. Bye for now."

Zara left the conversation.

"Well, I just wanted you to be the first to know. I love you. You still want to speak to Dad?" E. asked.

Ezra stepped into the picture and said, "Everything is okay, Julia. He's okay. It's late here, can we talk about this in the morning?"

"Yes. What time? Somewhere around 10:00 a.m. our time."

"Okay, I be waiting for your call."

"I love you, son," his mother said. "I suppose congratulations are in order."

"Thanks, Mom. Like Pop's mentioned, it's late here, and we all are tired."

"Alright, I expect to hear from you two tomorrow."

"Yes ma'am. Bye."

"Bye."

Julia hung up the phone, and her oldest son who was in the kitchen with her asked the million-dollar question: "Mom, did I hear Ezra tell you he is marrying a princess?"

"Yes, he did."

"No fair! He always has all the fun."

CHAPTER 04

$\mathcal{E}.$ and his father arrived back to their suite soon after the festivities ended. His father could tell that something was bothering him because of the way he slammed the door. He'd learned that it was best to approach things head on with his son.

He asked, "What's wrong?"

"Dad, what would make a man be so cold and calculating that he ties his daughter to a stranger? A foreigner, nonetheless."

"Son, things are done differently over here than in the states."

"You mean a woman doesn't have a right to dictate her future?"

"I believe that the country has progressed somewhat in its gender relations, but unfortunately the answer to that question is no. Zara has the additional burden of being a daughter to a very powerful king. Unfortunately, what she does is a direct reflection on the kingdom and her father. Oba Jaiye feels that he has her best interest at heart, and therefore he knows what's best for her, but it has to also be what's best for the kingdom."

"Then why would he want his daughter to marry a former coke head?"

"Oba Jaiye is a very wise man. He's able to look beyond someone's past and see that individual's future. You forget he knew your grandfather and me long before he knew you. He's seen what we have done with our lives, and he knows with the proper guidance you have the potential to be greater than us."

"So, you agree with him?"

"I don't agree with his methods all the time, but I know his heart. He would not have chosen you to be Zara's husband if he didn't believe you would be a good one. And yes, I believe this may be the best thing that ever happened to you in the long run." Ezra laughed. "Especially now that you've actually seen Princess Zara and know that she doesn't weigh three hundred pounds and have two missing front teeth."

E. rolled his eyes at his father.

"Oh, so you do like her?" Ezra asked raising his eyebrows. "... and I suppose you are physically attracted to her?"

"Yes, very much so. She is a stunning."

"My exact sentiments. Knowing Oba Jaiye, her mother was breathtakingly beautiful."

"I know, right?

Well, you've signed the betrothal agreement and the contract. It seems as though you're going to be a married man in about a year.

E. threw his head back in laughter.

Ezra reached out for his son's hand saying, "Son before we go to bed, let's have a moment of prayer."

E. nodded in agreement. Ezra began praying, "Father God..."

The comfort of her suite was a safe haven for a distressed princess. Her security guards saw her safely to her room. When the door closed, she crumbled to the floor, and the tears started. Vincent stepped out of the shadows and met her there. She was startled to feel his presence, but welcomed his tuxedo cladded shoulder for the reservoir of tears that she couldn't stop from flowing. They sat there until the sun came up. He encouraged her to get some rest and promised to come back that evening to have dinner with her and discuss the matter further. She agreed and crawled into her bed, gala gown and all. He covered her with a blanket, kissed on her forehead and bid her sweet dreams.

Zara woke up to the sound of humming birds outside of her bedroom window. At first her heart smiled. It was the simple things that brought her joy. She reached for her phone to start her mid-morning ritual with Victoria and noticed the kingdom news headlines announcing her betrothal. Memories of the unexpected life-changing event came crashing down on her. She covered her head with a pillow hoping that she could crawl back into dreamland. Then there was a hideous knock on her door. She was reluctant to answer it, but whoever it was was relentless.

"Princess Zara!" her assistant shouted from the other side of the door. "Your father has invited you for a late lunch. Your security detail will be here in an hour. Please let me in to prepare you."

Zara threw the pillow at the door, closed her eyes, and tried to think happy thoughts. Eventually she pulled herself out of the bed and opened the door for her assistant.

"Good morning, Camille."

"Congratulations, Princess Zara."

"Thank you, Camille. What can we do quickly to get me ready for this unexpected summons?"

"First let's get rid of this gown from last night. There's no time for a bath, so a quick shower will have to do."

Zara dropped the gown to the floor and rushed into the shower. Approximately forty-five minutes later, Princess Zara was dressed in a Dolce & Gabbana majolica print caftan with a matching turban, and large gold hoop earrings.

"Don't forget this," Camille said as she handed her the emerald cut Blue Nile four carat engagement ring. "It's very pretty."

"It is pretty, isn't it?" She sighed.

"Aren't you happy, Princess?"

"Oh, Camille, I had silly dreams of falling in love with my stunning chocolate prince riding in to rescue me on a white stallion."

"You don't think you can fall in love with him? I hear he's bad boy handsome. Somewhere between a Ryan Gosling and Chris Evans."

Zara gave Camille an astonished look.

"What?" Camille said. "You know news travels fast in the palace compound."

Zara laughed.

"Princess Zara, it's good to see you smile. Perhaps it's not as bad as you think. You might end up liking a man of a different flavor."

"That sounds like something Victoria might say. By the way, if she calls, tell her I will connect with her as soon as I can."

"Yes, Princess."

There was a robust knock on the door.

"My chariot awaits," Zara said before mumbling, "I wonder what else awaits me on the other side of this door."

Oba Jaiye's personal dwelling was a smaller mansion behind the main palace. It was almost two kilometers between the two, which usually required some mode of transportation. Zara was a little apprehensive about this meeting, especially after the previous night's events. Her kingdom duties required a lot of her, but it was the price she had to paid for her immeasurable access to anything in the world. In a perfect world she could have probably lived a normal life. But a normal life for a woman her age was that of a working mother in her kingdom. In that very moment she decided to be grateful for the life she has been given. Que sera sera.

The Range Rover pulled up in front of the king's residence, and Zara was greeted by his butler who directed her to the gardens. When she arrived, her father was seated with her betrothed and his father. Everyone except her father stood and greeted her. She was seated next to E.

Her father smiled and said, "You two look good together. It's better than I expected. Don't you agree Ezra?"

"Yes. But a marriage is built on so much more than good looks. Don't you agree Oba Jaiye?"

"Yes, I do. Spoken like a true man of wisdom." He looked at the young couple. "I called you here today to set the stage for your courtship. I am well aware that you don't know each other yet. So, this next week, before E. returns to America, I would like to see you two become more familiar with each other. I had my secretary set up a series of chaperoned events that will allow you the liberty to lay a strong relational foundation for your courtship. Zara, you put all palace, kingdom, and personal activities on hold until Ezra Jr. and his father leaves. When he returns, he will start his training as a royal. Agreed?"

Oba Jaiye looked at Ezra Sr. who nodded in agreement.

"Now, Ezra Sr. and I have some matters that we must discuss. We will leave you two to get better acquainted."

"Yes, Father."

Both men walk down the concrete path leading to the house and soon disappeared. The butler showed up with a hearty meal for Zara, and the kitchen cook brought a similar meal for E.

"These are the princesses favorite breakfast foods," the cook explained.

"Well, thank you Mary, I never expected such a feast the day after a gala."

"I'm sure everything is delicious." She turned to E. "Let's start orienting you to the Dala Dynasty culture. These are bambalouni; they are similar to American donuts. This is eggah, which is like your American omelet. And these are ewa which are similar to pinto beans in your country. Are you a foodie?"

"Yes, to a certain extent. We are from Houston, which is one of the most diverse cities in the United States. I love the fact that you can simply turn a corner and enjoy a popular cuisine from another country right there in the city limits. Have you ever been to Texas?"

"No."

"The United States?"

"No."

"Well, you must come to visit sometime."

"Absolutely. Let's enjoy the food before it gets cold."

"I'm starving, how about you?"

"Yes, but I must warn you once you eat one of Mary's bambalouni, you will never want another American donut ever."

The young couple commence to devour their midday meal with a reckless abandonment while their fathers are discussing their future.

The two older men were in the king's study that overlooked the garden. Each man had a drink of Redemption 36-Year-Old Bourbon in his hands.

"Oba Jaiye, Zara did not know about the betrothal?"

The king paused before he spoke. "No."

"Was that intentional, or is it your custom to handle arranged marriages that way?"

"It's actually up to the parent as to how the child finds out. I just wanted to share the good news with her and the world at the same time."

"Oba Jaiye, you forget I know you very well. The man I see sitting before me is not much different from the little boy I built a lifelong friendship with."

"Ezra, I forgot I could never get away with anything around you. So, what does it matter? She has adjusted well to the idea. Your boy seems to like her. I don't see that there's a problem."

"I do. I will not have my son in a loveless marriage—arranged or not. I've suffered through two divorces, and I wouldn't want anyone, not even my worst enemy, to experience what I went through."

"There will be no divorce. That's the whole purpose of the betrothal. My daughter will do what I tell her to do."

"Out of fear or love, Oba Jaiye?"

The king put his glass down on the table, and looked his friend in the eyes. "Zara was born a royal. Love has absolutely nothing to do with my decision. It is the best thing for the kingdom."

"How is that? Why isn't she marrying one of the sons of a chief from a local providence or another royal?"

"Because they are not good enough for her. She needs a man in her life that can lead and follow."

"How do you know that my son can do those things? Just a few months ago he was a womanizer and an addict."

The king laughed. "Ezra, I know you."

"I haven't been the best father to Ezra."

"I think you are being too hard on yourself. I've been observing you two since you got here. That boy loves you, and you love him."

"Yes. That's true."

"What do you American's say? 'Better late than never.'"

"Do you love Zara, Oba Jaiye?"

"Why would you ask me such an absurd question as that? She is my daughter and will rule my kingdom when I am with my forefathers. Is there a greater love than a man has for his kingdom?"

"Oba, you didn't answer my question."

"Yes, my friend, I did. You just may not have liked my answer."

Ezra took another drink of his bourbon.

"Now that we are clear on where I stand, do you still want your son to marry my daughter?"

Ezra sighed, "He seems to want to pursue this engagement. I will stand by whatever decision he makes. If this thing goes south, I expect you to do the honorable thing and release him from this agreement."

"No, Ezra, I will not willingly do that. This isn't America where you can arbitrarily say 'yes' to something one day and 'no' the next. What kind of king would my people consider me to be if I allowed that kind of behavior to prevail? Zara has been kept pure for her husband. My kingdom is offering your son a rare flower. He should not be taking it lightly."

"Oba Jaiye, I will not barter with my son's happiness."

"Then what else can you offer me in its place? Consider this dear friend: if we ever reach that crossroads where you must come up with a substitute, someone in your bloodline will marry my daughter, even if it has to be you."

The king rises from his chair and goes to the window that has a panoramic view of his garden. He spied the young couple eating breakfast.

He looked back at Ezra and said, "We will not speak of this again. I don't like disagreeing with you about anything, Ezra. My love for you runs deep, but my love for my kingdom runs deeper."

"I hear you, my brother. I hear you," Ezra replied. "But always remember, I too, am a man who loves his family just as much as you love your kingdom. I will hold you to the agreement that we made years ago not to bring harm to each other or anyone in our bloodline because of the unique friendship we share. To me those were more than mere words written by two teen boys who were on the brink of becoming men and seeking out their purpose. I believe God has brought us together again for a much higher purpose than either of us can possibly understand right now, and I leave the fate of our children in His hands, and the gates of Hell will not prevail against it."

Curiosity held the two young people in the garden for several hours. Initially they sought to find a bridge to foster their conversation, something that was common and familiar to both of them. Food seemed to be a great place to connect with one another.

"The food was delicious," E. said. "You seem to be well versed in American cuisine."

"Well yes," Zara said smiling. "Attribute it to my binging on the Master Chef with Gordon Ramsay."

They both laughed.

"Ezra, now that we've met, are you sure you want to go through with the courtship?"

"Why do you ask, Princess Zara? Oh, by the way, you can call me E."

"Oh, okay then, E. I asked the question because I don't believe in divorce."

"I see. Well, Princess Zara, I made a serious commitment to see this thing through. I signed the betrothal agreement fully aware of what was required of me."

"Have you ever dated an African or African-American woman before?"

"No."

"Interesting."

"But that doesn't mean it's not possible to love a woman from another race. My mother is actually married to an African-American former NFL player. So, I'm not a stranger to interracial relationships or marriage."

"The woman I met last night is married to a black man?"

"Yes. And I have four other brothers and sisters that look a lot more like you than me."

"So, what kind of women have you dated?"

"I'm a mama's boy, so I once preferred women who looked just like her."

"I see."

"But, I can tell you that when you walked down the aisle on the arm of your father, I was pleased with what I saw."

Zara blushed.

"And you," E. returned the question to Zara. "What kind of men are you use to dating?"

"None," Zara quickly replied. "My father has every single man in this kingdom under his spell. If anyone even looks at me, he might end up missing a few days later."

E. and Zara giggled.

"You are kidding, right?"

"No. Actually I'm not."

Ezra went to his room in the palace soon after his conversation with Oba Jaiye. He felt a need to pray more than he'd ever prayed in his life. Not for E. or Zara, or their relationship, but for his boyhood friend whose life was on the precipice of a downward spiral straight to the pit of hell.

He fell to his knees and prepared to pour out his heart: "Heavenly Father, it's me again... "

Zara and E. soon became like Siamese twins attached at the hip. The week had been a whirlwind of constant activities, events, and training. It was a crash course on getting to know each other.

It all started with a press conference with the African media and ended with time spent on an African Safari with exotic wildlife and the magic of the jungle captivating their imaginations. The king even brought in a consultant to administer a series of personality tests so that E. and Zara could better understand their personal strengths and weaknesses and properly communicate with each other as husband and wife based on their love languages. They also met with Cardinal Arinze to start their marital counseling sessions.

As Zara got to know E. better, she began to understand why her father chose him instead of someone local. He was confident, kind, and he didn't back down from a challenge. But most importantly, he was honest. He told her about his past as a prodigal and how his father helped him kick his addiction. She was compassionate and understanding, which was evidence of her maturity. E. was mystified by Zara. He'd never met a woman like her before in his life.

In the evenings they would either dine with their fathers at the king's mansion or with E.'s father at the palace. When the king was absent from their dinners, Ezra would share stories of their boyhood adventures with Zara and his son. She was so intrigued by their story that Zara arranged for them to take a field trip to the Holy Hill where the two had made a blood covenant.

Ezra would also talk with them about the lifelong work of his missionary ancestors around the world, particularly about their time on the African continent.

By the time of their last evening together before E. and his father were to return to America, the two of them had formed a budding friendship. The possibility of it blossoming into love was still in question, but there was definitely a mutual respect brewing.

On their last evening the couple had lunch with Oba Jaiye and Ezra in the garden. The roses were in full bloom, and their intoxicating scent heightened the garden experience. The nearby marble-tiered Versailles fountain was in full force. Its miniature waterfall effect set the perfect romantic setting.

The king had the chef cook American cuisine in honor of their guests. It was a steak and baked potato culinary adventure with all the toppings, authentic apple pie for dessert, and iced tea. The four discussed the young couple's future. Her father reiterated the importance of their courtship and preparation for a lifelong marriage. Zara was surprised because that hadn't been the pathway her father had taken. On the other hand, Ezra had been married twice, and neither marriage had lasted. It was evident that both men wanted the best for their children for different reasons, but the best nonetheless.

The men left Zara and E. in the garden to enjoy the rest of their time together and finish off that bottle of bourbon. It would be a long time before they saw each other again because Ezra had a business to rebuild, and the Oba Jaiye had a kingdom to run.

E. and Zara resumed their conversation about their childhood antics after the men left. They shared pictures from the early days late into the evening until it was time for E. and his father to go to the airport. The driver came to alert E. that they would be leaving soon.

Before he left, E. looked at Zara and grabbed the hand that housed her engagement ring. He got on his knees and said, "Princess Zara, I know that we have only known each other for a short period of time, but I want you to know that I am very serious about my commitment to you. Do you feel the same way?"

"Yes," she said looking into his eyes.

"Good."

He returned to his chair with a huge smile on his face and said, "So let the courtship begin."

"What did you think we were doing?" She asked.

"I didn't want to assume anything, especially because this whole thing was new to you. I assume your imaginary prince charming didn't look anything like me."

"You are very discerning."

"That's not what I asked."

"Actually, you didn't ask me a direct question."

"You are right," E. agreed. "Let me try another tactic. What did he look like?"

"Who?"

"Your imaginary prince charming? Did he look like Michael B. Jordan, Idris Elba, Common, Jesse Williams, or Morris Chestnut?"

"I noticed you didn't include any rappers or balladeers in the list like Big Sean, Drake, Travis Scott, Machine Gun Kelly, Usher or John Legend."

"I don't think you are the groupie type," he said while playfully drawing a heart on her arm.

"What type do you think I am?"

"Well, you might be the fangirling type."

"What's that?"

"It's someone who expresses excessive excitement over a person they might like."

"So, you envision me going wild if I were to see Idris Elba or Morris Chestnut?"

"Maybe."

"Well," she said, "I will have you to know that I have met both of them, and if I remember correctly, I was as cool as a cucumber…until they left. It was Victoria who almost fainted when she saw them."

They spent the rest of the evening laughing as they shared stories about meeting other famous people.

Oba Jaiye and Ezra said their goodbyes in his study over the last of the bourbon. During this trip, they learned that what they had as boyhood friends still remained. They were men now that must sometimes agree to disagree; however, their love for each other remained. Ezra was the last one to get into the sedan. He sat in the front with the driver to give the betrothed couple some alone time.

The moon was especially bright that night as they rolled down the highway toward the airport. E. reached over for Zara's hand and caressed her engagement ring finger.

"I will return in a few weeks, a month at the most, to start the training program your father designed for me," he said.

"You may want to get plenty of rest while you are there," Zara suggested. "You will need it."

"Really?"

"Yes."

"Why?"

"You'll see."

E. grabbed her hand and slowly ran his lips over the back of it. He released it when he saw the driver's eyebrow raising. He gently placed her hand back in her lap.

"You know what?" He whispered. "It'll be worth every second of it if in the end I can have you."

America wasn't Africa. It wasn't a place a proud African man could walk the streets without fear of being arrested, especially if he was carrying. Sarki found it strange to be in Texas, the home of the pistol-packing cowboys and rifle-toting farmers.

"And people are threatened by my mere presence?" Sarki thought to himself. He was ready to go home. Maybe checking up on what's happening at home would cure his longing for his motherland. He slipped into the business office at his Hyatt hotel where he'd been a resident for the last two weeks. The king was insistent that he do a thorough investigation of E. Johnson Construction's cyber security system, which required a personal visit to America. He would be called home any day now. It wouldn't be a minute too soon for him.

Sarki got as comfortable as possible in the worn office chair and started surfing the Internet for news and current events. After a few minutes of browsing, there on the front page of AllAfrica.com was the announcement of Princess Zara and E.'s betrothal. He slammed the mouse on the computer desk and pushed the computer on the floor in a fit of rage. Ten minutes later he was escorted from the hotel by security. Sixty minutes after that, he was boarding a flight for his native country.

"To hell with this American assignment!" Sarki thought.

He'd made up his mind and would deal with the king later. But not before he dealt with Zara. She would not be marrying the American, and if the king insisted, he could easily be handled. He was determined to have her, even if someone had to die to make it happen.

Eighteen hours later, he landed in the Dala Dynasty. It had taken all of his last month's salary to book a private flight home after arriving in Lagos. When he arrived at the palace compound, it was midnight. He immediately went to Zara's suite and assured the guards that he was there on a personal errand for the king. Though questionable, they let him in. Princess Zara was sound asleep after a tiring week of premarital preparations with E.

Sarki did a careful assessment of her apartment. It had been a while since he visited Zara. He regretted not taking advantage of the times he could have solidified their relationship. He sat in the chair beside her bed with a heavy heart for several hours watching her sleep and waiting for the changing of the guard. That's when he would make his move. If she decided to scream no one would be there to hear her. He wrestled between pretending to be an intruder and kidnapping her or just taking her right there in her bed while she was sleeping. He chose the latter strategy.

If she became pregnant as a result of his actions, the king would have to let them get married. He'd waited twenty-one years for her, and he would not be denied. Sure, there were other women in his life, but they'd meant nothing to him. She was his prize—the very reason for all the long working hours, rigorous training, and being at the beck and call of her insidious father twenty-four hours a day, seven days a week.

The liquor he brought on the airplane emboldened him. In it he found the courage to rightful claim his reward. He'd preferred her falling for him on her own accord, but that was now out of the question. He would have to force the matter if he was to be king of Dala Dynasty someday. She was his ticket to greatness. What would she know about ruling a kingdom? Zara would be mere putty in his hands. He would allow her to rule temporarily, but the day would come when the children would need their mother, and the silly girl would not be able to refuse making him king. He'd make sure of that. Rape hadn't been part of his plan, but desperate times required desperate action.

The king's mansion was deadly quiet. Oba Jaiye struggled to go to sleep, so he decided to visit his secret room to check on the status of the kingdom. When he got to the monitor that showed what was going on in his daughter's room, he was surprised to see a strange man sitting in the chair adjacent to her bed.

He immediately picked up the telephone and called the acting head of security and commanded that they rescue Princess Zara from the clutches of the intruder. He followed his command with a threat: if she was violated or harmed in any way, everyman on duty that night would pay with his life. The king grabbed his slippers and robe and alerted his driver to take him to the palace.

Vincent heard the distress call and was the first to the princess's apartment. The door had been locked from the inside, but he busted it down with the fury of a much younger man. The princess awoke suddenly when she heard the crash. The intruder was startled, but not enough to run away. He came charging at Vincent, and the two men both skilled in hand-to-hand combat went at each other with a fierceness that had a frightened Zara screaming to the top of her lungs. It soon became obvious that each man was willing to die before surrendering. Just when the younger man was getting the best of the older man in the battle a platoon of palace guards accompanied by the king rushed in the room and grabbed the intruder. It took four men to pull Sarki off of Vincent, who fell to the floor.

The king shouted, "Who would be insane enough to attempt to defile the princess? Surely you know that you signed your own death sentence. Turn on the lights you, imbeciles, so that we can see who this fool is."

When the bright lights from the chandelier pierced the darkness, it was apparent who the intruder was. Sarki stood there like a captured warrior.

Zara gasped.

Her father shook his head in disbelief before commanding his soldiers, "Take him to the palace prison. I will deal with him in the morning."

The flight attendant called their flight number over the intercom. After a few weeks of rest and family time, E. was going back to Africa to his princess. They had officially been engaged for almost a month now, and he still had a desire to see this thing through.

Little did he know, what was happening in the kingdom would not only drastically change his life, but that of his betrothed.

CHAPTER 05

The rumor of Sarki's betrayal filled the Dala Dynasty's airways. Oba Jaiye held a press conference to alleviate the rumors and assure his people due to the sensitivity of the matter, that his former head of security would be tried by a group of his peers. Earlier that morning Sarki's father visited and begged that his son's life be spared. The king was known for his swiftness in handling matters of this nature, but he was moved by the compassionate plea of his father, a former childhood friend.

At that moment Sarki had other plans. He still had friends within the security force who were more loyal to him than the kingdom, and with their help he escaped. That evening the main accomplice who assisted in his escape was hung in the middle of the palace compound. A bounty for one million dollars was placed on Sarki's head that evening.

The palace announcement read:

Sarki Acheampong Wanted: Dead or Alive

Reward $1,000,000

The limousine pulled up to the palace gates, and the driver took the long way around to the palace. It was a more scenic route, but E. was concerned about the change. He questioned the driver about it. To E.'s disappointment, the driver informed him that they were going to the king's mansion instead of the palace compound. When E. got out of the car, to his surprise, he was greeted by Oba Jaiye. To the king's surprise, E. had an unannounced companion with him, his mother. He was obviously shocked.

"Oba Jaiye, this is my mother, Julia Washington Barnes."

She curtsied, "Your Highness," she said as she rose, "I couldn't let my son make such a life-changing decision without my approval. After all he is a momma's boy, aren't you honey?"

"Mom, you're embarrassing me before the king."

Oba Jaiye quickly recovered his composure and immediately became the consummate host.

"Well, greetings my beautiful guest. For a moment I thought Ezra was bringing a younger sister to enjoy the pleasures of my palace," the king said smiling.

"Oba Jaiye, I see why you and E.'s father are the best of friends; you both are charmers."

The king grabbed her hand and kissed it. "Ezra was a fool to let you get away. If you were mine, you would never have escaped me."

"Unfortunately, I am very married and the mother of five. My husband would tear down that beautiful palace gate to return me to his arms and my motherly duties," she laughed.

Oba Jaiye turned to E., "Does the princess know that your mother is here?"

"No. I wasn't able to reach her before we boarded the plane."

"Well, let's get you comfortable," the king said to Julia, "and I will place more guards on the gate just in case your husband decides to come for a visit."

He gently took her arm and escorted her into the palace.

The king retired to his chambers after he was assured that his guest were well taken care of. He called Vincent to his room.

Vincent entered, "Your Highness, you called?"

"I need you to take care of that body that is flailing in the palace square," the king sternly said. "We have American guests, and they have a sensitivity to seeing dead bodies blowing in the wind. Bury him as far as possible from the palace and relocate his widow and children to another African village with a monthly allowance. I need this problem to disappear quickly. Am I understood?"

"Yes, Your Highness."

"I also need your assurance that the princess will be back to her old self to entertain our guests. You seem to have a way with her."

"Yes, Your Highness."

"Have her ready by dinner."

"Yes, Your Highness."

"And, thank you for taking over as my temporary head of security. My gratitude will be reflected in your monthly allowance."

"Sir, there was no need to do that because I..."

Oba Jaiye interrupted Vincent. "You are refusing a gift from your king?"

"No sir."

"Good. I'll see you at dinner with the princess."

"Yes sir."

The kingdom maids and movers came to relocate her to another suite in the center of the palace. She'd spent the afternoon in the office of the kingdom psychiatrist discussing the previous night's events. Once released, she was escorted back to her new apartment. It was bigger than her previous home, but more secure. Her father was known as the most security-conscious king in all of Africa. She was safe if nothing more. Her heart was broken though. Someone who was near and dear to her had betrayed her, and she was shattered. It took her all morning to find a semblance of normalcy.

She expected to hear from Victoria, but her telephone had been confiscated. Maybe she could explain why Sarki would want to hurt her in that way. Perhaps she had tempted him with her flirtations on the way home from college, but he had showed absolutely no evidence of his interest. By now, he would probably be dead. There were too many unanswered questions with no answers. She was getting a migraine trying to figure it all out. Just as she was reaching for the Zolmitriptan, Vincent knocked on the door.

"Princess Zara, it's Vincent."

"Thank God. Finally. Come in."

"Are you okay?" He asked while limping across the threshold of her suit. "Duty called, so I had to come check on you."

"How did you know to come to my room last night to rescue me?"

"Your father called the security staff to your room."

"How did he know Sarki was in my room?"

"Zara, you know your father. He has eyes everywhere."

"But Sarki was his head of security; shouldn't he have known better?"

"Obviously, he didn't."

"Is he dead, Vincent?"

"No, Princess. Sarki has escaped."

"What? Oh my god. That's why I was moved this morning."

"Yes. But don't worry your father has this place locked down tighter than a pregnant elephant's stomach."

Zara smiled.

"Listen my princess, Sarki wouldn't dare come within 100 miles of this compound. If he does, someone is going to be $1,000,000 richer."

"What? Father put a bounty on his head?"

"Yes."

"Vincent, what if he is suffering some kind of mental illness?" Zara asked searching to find a valid reason for Sarki's irrational actions. "He can't be held accountable for what he did if he wasn't in his right mind."

"Well princess whether he was or not, he is now an enemy to the Dala Dynasty. Remember, 'He who digs a grave for his enemy might as well be digging one for himself.'"

"Sarki is gone to us forever then, Vincent?" Zara asked sadly before hanging her head down. Tears ran run down her cheeks.

"Yes, my princess. But let's talk about something else," Vincent quickly changed the subject. "Your father has invited you to dinner, so have your assistant prepare you. Be ready at 7:00 p.m. Your security detail will be here at 6:45 p.m. to pick you up."

He turned her face toward him and said, "Promise me you will put all of this behind you?"

"I will try."

"Good." He kissed her on the forehead and left her staring out of the window, mourning the absence of her best friend and her cousin. Kingdom life could be lonely sometimes, especially when you're destined to someday be its ruler.

The chandeliers glistened and rivaled the brilliance of the Lenox silverware. The table was perfectly set in the Great Room for its esteemed guests. The king met E. and his mother in the hallway and escorted them to dinner. When they arrived, a bedazzled Zara was sitting at the table wondering why there were three additional place settings on the table. Her father and Julia were the first to enter the room. The princess rose out of respect for her father and greeted him first. The woman looked vaguely familiar, but Zara didn't want to appear pretentious, so she remained quiet while her father introduced their guest.

"Zara, this is Julia Washington Barnes. She is an American who has come unexpectedly to our glorious kingdom."

"Good evening, Mrs. Washington Barnes. It's my pleasure to make your acquaintance."

Her father pulled out Julia's chair then sat down in his at the head of the table. Once he was seated, he rang a bell.

Julia started asking Zara questions about the weather and the palace compound as a means to distract her from E. entering the room dressed as a server. He brought her salad, placed it next to her and asked, "Will there be anything else ma'am?" She instantly recognized the voice and turned to locate its owner. There stood E. with a huge smile on his face. She forgot palace decorum and literally jumped into his arms. As he embraced her, she began to weep.

Between her sobs, she whispers into E.'s shoulder, "Dara julo."

He looked at her father and asked, "What is she saying?"

He smiled and responded, "She is calling you her best friend."

"Princess, are you okay?"

The king responded, "Of course, she is. Zara, we have guests. Compose yourself."

She mumbled an apology to E. and Julia.

E. asked her if she was ready to go back to her seat. She nodded yes.

E. gently led the princess back to her chair and kneeled beside her declaring, "I missed you too, Zara."

Her maidservant came to the opposite side of her chair, handed her a box of tissues, and waited for the young princess to request her assistance. Instead, Zara, excused herself, promising to return in a few minutes. An awkward silence filled the room until the princess reappeared.

After a brief trip to the powder room, the princess returns as immaculate as she was before the guests arrived for dinner.

She apologized to her father for her emotional outburst and attributed it to the weight of the unexpected surprise. He reassured her that he understood and recognized the blossoming love between the young couple. He added that the best place to start in building a solid relationship is friendship. He turned to Julia for her acknowledgment, which she freely gave.

E. reached for Zara's hand under the table and squeezed it for reassurance. His mother was amazed at the tenderness her son shared with the young princess. She'd never seen him express his affection in that way toward anyone except her and his siblings. She felt a pang of jealousy, but quickly pushed it away because what she was seeing in front of her was an answer to prayer.

E. then introduced his mother to Zara. The princess blushed when Julia grasped her hand and said, "So, you are the woman who has my son's heart. We've met before on FaceTime, but it's an honor to meet you in person. He's right; he has really missed you. The pilot couldn't fly the plane fast enough."

The small assembly of dinner guests laughed. Vincent entered the room and acknowledged the king and the princess. E. rose to shake his hand, and the king bid him to sit in the vacant chair. He introduced Vincent to Julia as his interim head of security and Zara's baba ninuun Kristi. He explained that those words mean godfather in American English.

The king expressed his desire for Julia to meet the important people in Zara's life because of the upcoming nuptials. She acknowledged the importance of family and explained that was the reason for her visit. She understood that E. was a grown man capable of making his own decisions, but marriage blended families, and everyone involved needed to at least know each other. The king agreed.

Zara couldn't believe the metamorphosis that had occurred in her father; he was actually charming and freely shared stories about his many trips to America and the time he'd spent as an intern at an American corporation. Some of these stories she heard for the very first time. The evening went on well past the dessert.

They retired to the king's elegant sitting room where he met with dignitaries from other countries. It was a very large traditional room with several chocolate sofas and loveseats, and orange accent chairs, with huge handmade area rugs from India that complemented the decor. It was also the place where the king showcased his favorite artwork, particularly the work of Sudanese artist Ibrahim El-Salahi. E. sat close to Zara listening quietly as the senior adults conversed.

Zara was shocked when the king encouraged Vincent to share stories of their long history with Zara. The atmosphere was cheerful until Julia mentioned Zara's mother. The king simply said she died soon after childbirth, and he had raised the princess with the help of his staff and respected educators in the UK. He asked Vincent to share what he knew about Zara's mother as a little girl because they were from the same village.

Hesitantly, Vincent began to share his memories of her. He first talked about her beauty as a child and how she was known in the village as the "Omo Iewa" because she was not only beautiful outside but also inside. "Wherever she went, she was followed by a sweet aroma," Vincent said with great heart and expression. "When she matured into her womanhood, she'd grown even lovelier. The chief of his village had great expectations for her because she possessed an innate innocence and an unfathomable hope. One day the prince was passing by a stream where the women bathed after a hard day's work. He saw her, and her beauty captivated him. He proposed on the spot. After giving her father and the chief a hefty bride price, the prince carried her off to his kingdom. Zara is the result of their short-lived romance."

Everyone was mesmerized by Vincent's narrative because he was a master storyteller. Julia thanked him for sharing and offered her sincere condolences to the king. He thanked her for her kindness and said that it was well past his bedtime. He had to retire soon. Julia asked if she could spend some time with Zara before she left, and the king obliged. He rang for his manservant and informed him to take Julia's things to the princess' apartment. She would now be staying with her for the duration of the trip. Julia started to correct the king and inform him of his misinterpretation of her intent, but E. shook his head, no.

Within the hour everyone was snuggled securely underneath Down comforters on one thousand-count thread sheets—Julia in a room in Zara's apartment and E. at the king's mansion. Zara mused over the day's events and realized that she had learned more about her mother on that evening than she had in her entire lifetime.

Zara was meeting with her personal assistant in her office when Julia dragged in—no makeup, hair akin to a blonde mop, and PJs that screamed busy Mom. She was a hot mess first thing in the morning.

"Good morning, Julia," Zara said. "How did you enjoy your rest?"

"I think the jet lag has finally gotten the best of me," Julia responded. "If it wasn't for my husband and kids calling me, I would probably still be asleep. She flopped down in an office chair beside Zara's desk. I dreamed that I was floating around on a cloud visiting all the places that I've ever wanted to go to."

"Wow! Well, I am glad that you got some rest," Zara said while signaling for her assistant to leave. She turned to Julia and asked, "What would you like to do today after brunch?"

"Brunch? It's that late? Umm, I can have anything I want for breakfast?"

"Yes," Zara said as she dialed the phone. "Good morning, chef. Our guest would like to make a request for breakfast." She handed the phone to Julia.

"Hi," Julia said, "I would like to have a Texas omelet fully loaded with a side of hash browns, biscuits, a fruit salad, and the biggest glass of orange juice possible. It'll be ready in sixty minutes? Great. Thanks. Before my food gets here, I have time to take a bath and get gorgeous," Julia said after hanging up the phone. "What do you do during the day?"

"I have a weekly and daily agenda that outlines my kingdom duties. Today, I am scheduled to visit the Royal Stables to show some of our doctors the value of equestrian therapy when dealing with troubled youth. Do you ride?"

"Yes. It's been awhile though."

"I will have my assistant bring you something to ride in. You're an eight?"

"Yes."

"Enjoy your brunch."

Two hours later Julia was in the stable in the background listening to her future daughter-in-law show several doctors the magic of equestrian therapy. She was impressed. This young woman may be seven years younger than her son, but she was definitely his equal when it came to maturity. She was articulate, beautiful, and kind. But something was missing? She couldn't quite put her finger on it yet. Before she left, she would definitely know what it was. Her son's future depended on it.

Zara was well aware of Julia's presence in the stables. She decided to focus on her presentation instead of worrying about her future mother-in-law. When the class was over, she answered some questions from the participants and joined Julia soon after.

"Are you ready for our ride?" Zara asked.

"Yes," Julia replied. "Do I get to pick my horse?"

"Absolutely."

A few minutes later they began touring the property with three palace security agents following closely behind them. Julia picked a chestnut Barb with a beautiful flowing mane. Zara was riding a blue roan Nooitgedachter that stood majestically above the rest of the horses because of his height. The women began their adventure with a casual conversation.

"Zara, do these men follow you everywhere?"

"Yes."

"How do you deal with that?"

"I don't have a problem with it because it's been that way all of my life."

"Tell me a bit about yourself."

"There's not much to know that you haven't already heard. I've spent most of my life in the compound or away at school. My training to be a royal began as soon as I could walk. My father ensured that I had a well-rounded education and everything a girl could ever want."

"Do you have friends?"

"That list is very short, but my best friend is a schoolmate that I met in primary school named Victoria. My father saw that we got along quite well, and he paid for her to have the same quality education that I had. We've been friends for most of my life."

"I see. And how do you feel about being a royal?"

"I know no other lifestyle. I've been exposed to many things as a result of my privilege, but I do my best to pay it forward by bringing what I've learned back to my people as my father has done during his reign as king."

"Your father didn't remarry?"

Zara giggled. "My father has had many wives."

"Really?"

"Yes."

"None of them adopted you?"

"That wasn't the purpose of his marriages."

"I see."

"Julia," Zara said before asking a question. "May I ask you why you are here?"

"Honestly, I needed to see for myself what my son had gotten himself into." Julia replied before asking another question. "Why do you want to marry my son, Zara?"

Zara smiled and said, "He's funny, caring, kind and has a big heart."

"Do you know he's just recently gotten...?

"Sober?" Zara finished Julia's sentence. "Yes, I know."

"That doesn't matter to you?"

"It does, but he matters more."

"You've only known him for a little over a month. Have you ever been in love before?"

"Yes."

"With who?"

"This kingdom."

"Loving a man is quite different from loving a kingdom," Julia said. "Is there room in your heart to really love my son and your duties as a royal? He needs a wife, Zara, not necessarily a princess. Can you be a wife to my son? Do you even know what that means?"

"I can learn, Julia. I will learn!" Zara turned her horse around and shouted over her shoulder, "It's time to return home. We don't want to be late for dinner."

Julia was surprised at how abruptly their conversation ended, but she wasn't through with her investigation by a long shot.

Oba Jaiye was finishing a conference session with his staff when he found Julia sitting in the outer office. It was obvious that she wanted to speak with him. The week had been a series of events that involved her and the betrothed young couple. He was aware that she left E.'s room late yesterday evening after having a robust conversation about the marriage. He wondered if that had anything to do with her sitting there. She asked him if he had a few minutes to discuss the betrothal. He took her into his office after asking his assistant to hold all of his calls. She didn't waste time getting to the point.

"Oba Jaiye, I've spent the last week with my son and your daughter, and I am convinced that there is great potential there, but I have my concerns."

"Please feel free to share what's on your heart," the king said as he sat in the chair adjacent to Julia. "Now, I know my son is no choir boy," she reminded the king. "But I'm really concerned. I can tell that he is falling in love with Zara, and I don't want him to be put in a position for a setback if this relationship doesn't work out."

The king leaned forward. "Is there more?" He asked.

"Yes," she replied. "Your daughter has absolutely no idea about what is required of a wife. There are certain things that a woman learns when she has a role model, and Zara hasn't had that experience."

"She will in time," the king replied.

"That's what Zara told me," Julia said. "But, if I'm honest, my biggest fear is the kingdom will keep her from being a true wife to E."

The king pointed to the example of Britain's Queen Elizabeth and her husband Prince Philip. "They were married for seventy-four years and had a stable relationship, each of them falling deeper in love with each other as the years went by," he said. "Your son and my daughter will not be alone. I assure you that everyone in the palace compound is focused on making sure that this marriage is successful. In fact, that's what E.'s training program is about. It would acclimate him to the Dala Dynasty way and equip him to be a royal.

The king further addressed Julia's concern. Since she saw Zara's lack of preparation to be a wife a deterrent to their marital agreement, then Zara too would be placed in a training program. By making that comparison, the king evened the playing field and rendered Julia's objections fixable. He called his assistant and asked Julia what was her availability for the rest of the day. She said she was free after lunch. He told her he would meet her in the conference room to interview candidates to mentor Zara. Julia was flabbergasted. All she could do was nod in agreement to the king's plan as he escorted her from his office.

Three hours later E., and Julia were seated with the king in his conference room. The hallway was full of middle-aged, matronly-looking women. They interviewed candidates well into the evening and agreed to return in the morning to pick the top three candidates. E. and Zara had dinner alone in the king's dining area. He had been called away unexpectedly on kingdom business. Julia had her dinner brought to her room. She was exhausted.

"What's going on?" Zara asked E.

"My mother made mention to your father that you may need some help in becoming a wife. So, he had us interviewing several women that are known as good wives from the compound."

"What?" Zara exclaimed, followed by a robust burst of laughter.

E. said, "It's not funny. He was asking all kind of embarrassing questions that made several of the women blush. And they couldn't refuse to answer them because he is the king."

"That sounds like him."

"Are you offended?"

"No. Your mother expressed her concern to me earlier today. I'm more concerned about what you think. Do you think that I'm good wife material?"

"Of course, I do. And what you don't know, we can find out together."

"Why didn't you say that to your mother?"

"Because she and your father both want us to have a successful marriage. That's why they are investing so much in it and us. Considering that the statistics say that we have a fifty percent chance for success without the training, why not increase our odds for success with it?"

"You make a good point."

To her surprise, Zara was invited to the selection process. She couldn't believe that her father was using a democratic process to determine who her mentor would be. He was truly a totalitarian at heart. The change was remarkable to say the least.

The four of them sat in her father's cushy office chairs at an elegant oak table that ran the length of the room, waiting for the first candidate. Her father turned to her and said, "You and E. have a total of one vote toward the final decision. Julia and I, as parents, each have a vote."

His assistant passed out instructions for the interview, each of the candidate's bios and the investigations done by security. The kitchen staff brought in coffee and Chin Chin, Sfenji and Moin Moin with fresh juice for the interviewers. As they studied each candidate carefully, there was limited discussion. The king then asked everyone to rank each candidate based on preference from their individual review. After the interviewers prioritized their selections, they began the interview. The king presented each candidate with three main questions:

Why was being a good wife important?

What has been your most memorable experience as a wife?

What is your definition of a good marriage?

Each interviewee did a stellar job, but there was one that stood out above the rest. She was a portly woman with a pretty cocoa-colored face and thick gray braids with a smile that was enduring and welcoming. She was pleasantly warm, but confident. Flexible, but strong, and she fit the king's agenda perfectly. It was also the unanimous decision of the committee to hire her.

The king held a press conference the next day announcing the palace's new Iya for Princess Zara in preparation for her June wedding. Julia left for home the next day satisfied that her son was in good hands and that Princess Zara had the potential to be the wife her son needed. With her she took a farewell gift from the king, a beautiful Luxe diamond eternity necklace in eighteen carat white gold, a down payment on the dowry, and a suitcase full of souvenirs for her children. When she was safely on the Dala Dynasty private jet, the king looked at Vincent and said, "Let the courtship begin."

Boxes and crates were everywhere in Zara's suite. They had arrived early that morning from the coastal village of Tanit, the homeland of the Iya. The Iya, Ebunoluwa, was contracted to live with Zara for a total of six weeks. She was on duty during the week from sunrise to sunset, from Monday to Friday and returned home on the weekends to be with her family. Zara was scheduled to meet the Iya after lunch.

She'd spent several days trying to reach out to Victoria, but she received absolutely no response. In the eighteen years of their friendship, this had never happened. Zara pondered the possibility that perhaps her encounter with the now missing Sarki had severed their friendship. The thought was too much of a burden to bear.

The palace therapist had helped her deal with the traumatic attack, but her heart still cried out for an explanation. What compounded her inner dilemma was she had been firmly instructed by her father not to speak of the incident with E. or his mother for fear it would send him packing and on the next plane back to America. Zara had reluctantly agreed, but right about now she needed a friend, someone close to confide in.

It was drawing close to the time she was to meet with her new Iya. There was evidence in her suite that she had a new roommate, but Zara had been kept busy by the king with an early morning meeting about the betrothal with E.

The king laid out new additional guidelines that included the role of her Iya. E. in turn would begin his tour of the African continent which would conclude with a Rite of Adulthood in Cameroon. The young couple was shocked with the aggressive schedule and openly wondered about the king's intent. He responded with finality that his new son-in-law needed a crash course in their culture, and she needed an uninterrupted crash course in preparation to be a wife and how to master marital relationships. He reminded them that they both agreed to do what was best to create an atmosphere that was conducive for a successful marriage. He instructed them to prepare to say their good byes. It was only a temporary situation. They would be married soon enough and spend a lifetime together. Dinner tonight would be their last formal meeting.

The king had spoken, and when that happened it was considered the law in Dala Dynasty. E. reached out and took Zara's hand under the table and squeezed it to assure her that everything was going to be alright. This was becoming a common practice for the two of them. The king left the room after his pronouncement, and his manservant soon returned with an invitation for them to have lunch in the garden. They spent that time discussing their plans for communicating during the next six weeks.

Neither party was anxious to part when it was time for her to meet Ebunoluwa. But duty called. They'd been so engrossed in their conversation that she forgot to ask E. his thoughts on the matter of the matron. She reconciled herself with the thought that she would see him later that evening, and it would be one of the many things on the list of important topics for them to discuss

Ebunoluwa waited for her in her office in the suite. Zara remembered the genteel nature of this pleasant woman when Ebunoluwa greeted her with a smile. She stood as the princess entered the room, but Zara assured her that palace formalities were not necessary in her suite. She returned to her chair. Zara sat across from her at the small oak table in the conference room. Zara asked Ebunoluwa if she had completed her move. Ebunoluwa assured her that everything was in its place, and she was ready to start the training. Ebunoluwa asked if she could start their discussion in prayer. Zara found this unusual but bowed her head in agreement, as her new Iya prayed:

> *Dear Heavenly Father,*
>
> *As we start this journey, please send your Holy Spirit to lead us to the hidden treasures that you have vested in your princess and grant me the wisdom of Naomi as I mentor this young woman in the art of matrimony. May all that we do please you and glorify your kingdom. In Jesus' name, Amen.*

Ebunoluwa reached out to touch Zara's hand, encompassing her smaller one in her larger plump weathered hand. She looked deeply in the eyes of the princess and said, "For the next six weeks, it will be my honor to be your Iya. I know you lost your precious mother soon after birth, and in no way can I take her place."

She then pointed to Zara's heart with her other hand and said, "But it is my intent to help you fill that vacancy in here with a love that is much greater than a mother's love; it is the love of God that will make you the wife that He has called you to be!"

"I am merely an instrument or tool that He will use to do the necessary work to equip you for your heavenly kingdom purpose. My will is to please the heart of the heavenly Father in all that I do, and He has purposely assigned me to you. You are an orphan no more."

Tears begin to fall one by one on the conference table from the brown shaped ovals that belonged to one of Dala Dynasty's finest gifts. As each one reached its destination, God began to collect them and place them in a bottle of remembrance for all of Heaven to recall the day that Princess Zara took notice of a power that was greater than her earthly father's and a kingdom that was greater than Dala Dynasty. God was after her heart, and He would not stop until He possessed all of it.

There were rumors in the palace compound that Sarki had been sighted in Lagos. The king immediately dispatched his finest undercover agents to investigate the claim. The largest city in all of Africa was too close to home. If he was headed back this way, he had a plan to do serious damage to the king and his kingdom. The king was musing over Sarki's next move when he decided that extra security was required for him and the princess.

After an extensive investigation the king had learned of Sarki's intent to be king someday by marrying his daughter. He laughed at Sarki's pretentious assumption. He would have never allowed it because of the man's bloodline. The difference between Sarki and E. as a potential husband was massive. There was absolutely no way to justify a marriage between the former head of security and Zara, even if she had chosen him. His family wasn't wealthy. They weren't directly related to any one of the king's ancestors, maternal or paternal.

But E., on the other hand, had been engrafted into his bloodline through the covenant relationship that he had formed with Ezra during their childhood. He was a seed in his father's reproductive organs that had yet to be sown when they formed their covenant, but he was still there nonetheless. Their blood oath covered everything from that moment moving forward until one of them died. Even then, if their offspring decided to continue the covenant they could. The marriage between E. and Zara would ensure that his bloodline would continue and that Ezra and his family would be connected forever.

The king could see the love blossoming between Ezra Jr. and Zara. He'd made the right choice for his kingdom. The fact that Zara was happy was secondary. Sarki had a lifetime to convince Zara of his intentions, but failed. Then, here this American came, and in two short months swept her off of her feet, which solidified his plans for finding an appropriate suitor for Zara. The gods might finally be smiling on him.

He would delay his celebration until they were able to rid the kingdom of this vermin called Sarki. Then they all could live happily ever after in the kingdom Oba Jaiye built.

That evening Zara shared the details of her Iya encounter with E. He shared his "come to Jesus" moment on his father's boat with her. She left their discussion saddened by his departure in the morning but encouraged by his honest genuine testimony. He told her that praying for her and their relationship would continue to be a priority for him during his absence.

They spent the night long after dessert discussing their plans for the future and solidifying their commitment to each other. E. had only kissed Zara on her hand or cheek. He didn't want to rush their intimacy. His priority was to stay true to his commitment to remain celibate during their courtship, but he felt it was time for them to take it to the next level, and he wanted to give her something to remember.

The king found them there gazing in each other's eyes embracing after E. tattooed his unbridled passion on the lips of the princess. The king was immediately glad that miles and miles of African roads would soon be separating. He announced his presence and dismissed both of them to their separate bed chambers, but not after announcing that from this moment on they would be chaperoned when in each other's presence. Not even this impromptu decision could damper their enthusiastic love. They both reconciled that however long the wait was before they would feel the tenderness of each other's lips, it was worth it.

Oba Jaiye was not happy with the report that his men brought him about Sarki's second narrow escape. This derelict seemed more slippery than an eel, the king mused. The million-dollar bounty had been increased to two million, yet there was still no evidence that they were any closer to capturing him. This time his soldiers would know that their very lives depended on their success. He refused to grant a leave of absence to anyone until they found this culprit. Perhaps he would get some results now. One thing he hated more than anything else was incompetence.

With all of his secret service out looking for Sarki, he was limited to his personal security. Zara had none. He would have to remedy that soon. His council of elders reminded him that there was a group of women warriors who were regarded as some of the most ferocious combatants in all of Africa. The Alagbatas were a tribe of women warriors in Sudan from the Nubian tribe. They were similar in nature to the Dahomey Amazons except they were allowed to marry and have children.

The king dispatched a group of emissaries to the Saharan desert to locate the last remaining tribe of the Alagbatas. He summarized that he wouldn't have the concern of a male interloper plucking the flower princess before her time, and she would have the much-needed protection she required. The emissaries were instructed to offer seven single women warriors an annual salary of $100,000 and free room and board in the palace compound for a year with the opportunity for one-million-dollar bonuses if the palace compound or the princess's suites were breached by intruders. If for some reason they were killed in combat, but maintained the compound, their families would still receive the money.

When they located the village, there were literally hundreds of candidates. They decided to host a military competition, and the top winners would return to Dala Dynasty. The seven single women selected could have been competitors in the Africa Military Games; their skills and military acumen were unrivaled. Their sisters bid them a tearful farewell, and the king sent helicopters to return them and the emissaries back to the palace compound.

The Alagbatas were welcomed to the compound at the king's residence. He talked with them extensively about his expectations. They were also alerted to the situation with Sarki and its status. Each woman was outfitted with a military flight suit, khaki tops and bottoms, boots, and an arsenal of weapons to begin her service. They were also given a tour of the palace compound by Vincent.

The Alagbatas would be staying in the palace with Princess Zara in a suite adjacent to hers. Their suite had been prepped with security cameras and an armory. In each individual room there was a bed, a dresser, a walk-in-closet, a telephone, and a big screen television. There were three full bathrooms with all the amenities of the modern world in their suite. The ladies were amazed at the generosity of the king.

They slept like babies until 4:30 am when each woman was drugged with a shot of Propofol, blindfolded, cuffed, and thrown into the back of a sedan. They each awoke in a different part of the back country, miles apart from each other. Within twenty-four hours, each one of them had returned to the compound to the pleasure of the head of security. Vincent was pleased with their resilience. Because Nafisa was the first one to return to the compound, the king had selected her as the leader and spokesperson for the group. They were now ready to meet the princess of Dala Dynasty.

Zara and Ebunoluwa were sitting down to breakfast when the kitchen staff added eight more place settings to the table. The women looked at each other wondering what was about to take place. Obviously, they were expecting seven mystery guests. Several stately women soon joined them accompanied by Vincent who introduced them as Zara's new security staff. They kneeled before the princess who told them to rise and take their seats. Vincent introduced them. Their names were: Aarifa, Fazilah, Hiba, Leila, Nafisa, Tiwa and Yaya.

Each woman was asked to tell why she had chosen to be a woman warrior and why had she selected this assignment. Nafisa was the first to offer her explanation. Her father was a merchant in their village, and she was the thirteenth child of twenty, 19 girls and one boy. When it came time for his only son to perform his military service, her father felt that he was more valuable as an heir to his business and offered her to take his place as an Alagbatas. She selected this assignment because she was adventurous and had always been curious about Dala Dynasty. Her family's business fell on hard times, and she wanted to help her father restore his business to its former glory.

The next person to tell her story was Leila. Her family had been the victims of a tribal civil war, and she was orphaned at an early age. She chose to become an Alagbata because she wanted to bring honor to her family name. She volunteered for this assignment because it would bring further honor to her lineage.

Aarifa spoke next. Most of her family had died of AIDS. She'd lived in the streets for most of her childhood. One night the police picked her up from the streets for trespassing, and the magistrate gave her the option of being thrown in jail for a year or becoming an Alagbata warrior after the police described the arduous chase that took placed when they were trying to apprehend her. She was the fastest woman in her village and in the chaperones and could outrun a cougar if necessary. She'd chosen this assignment because it would be the first place that she could spread her wings of independence.

Yaya shared her story after Aarifa finished. She'd come from a village of farmers and gotten bored with that lifestyle. She sought an opportunity to fine tune her skills as a warrior.

Hiba had a similar story, but her family was impoverished to the point where they had started to sell off the children as indentured servants to neighboring farms. She ran away before it was her turn. The Alagbata found her dying in the desert. They rescued her, and one of the women adopted her as her own child. She chose this assignment because she wanted to make her predecessor proud.

Tiwa was next to tell her story. She'd been captured by pirates to be sold in Sudan to the highest bidder. She faked sickness to be brought to a local hospital where she escaped her captors. She wandered into the Alagbata's camp one night when she was about to die of starvation. She was seduced by this mission because of the pay and the opportunity to start a new life.

Last but not least, Fazilah shared her story. She had heard the village griots share the stories of the Alagbata warriors and yearned to become one as a young girl. When she came of age to make that decision, she alerted the chief in her village, and he gave her safe passage to their camp as a gesture of good will. She had envisioned her spending the rest of her life in that camp, but was enticed when the opportunity to serve a real princess was presented to her tribe. Her goal was to be one of the best warriors for the princess that there ever was.

Princess Zara enthusiastically welcomed each of the ladies and introduced her Iya. They went on to enjoy their breakfast in a pleasant silence, each wondering what the future would bring.

Vincent stuck around after breakfast to bring Zara up to date on her security protocol. He sat down in the chair adjacent to hers and shared the current news about Sarki and her father's concern. She now understood the reason for the new security team.

"Do you have news of Victoria?" Zara asked. "I am concerned about her."

Vincent hesitated. "Your father has banned all of Sarki's family members from the palace compound and stopped all means of communication with them. They are under house arrest until he is found."

Zara was saddened by this news. Looking for a pleasant diversion she asked, "Have you heard anything about E.'s trip?"

He smiled and said, "So you miss your betrothed."

"Yes, I do. You know me too well."

"My precious princess," he said, "you will soon see your beloved. In the meantime, you will be preparing for that glorious day all safe and sound in the comfort of the palace compound."

"…under the watchful eye of my Iya and the Alagbata warriors," Zara added.

CHAPTER 06

Dala Dynasty was an especially beautiful place in the summer. The fragrant exotic flowers drew many of its inhabitants outside of the palace walls and with that excursion came a brief visit to paradise. The king was out on a goodwill mission exploring the southernmost part of his kingdom.

Zara and Ebunoluwa sat in the palace garden enjoying the beauty of the day preparing for the first session of what was now being called the Bridal Bootcamp. Ebunoluwa brought several books to the table. One of them was the Bible. It was a sight for sore eyes with its worn brown cover, torn spine, faded "Books of the Bible" tabs, and numerous highlights that seemed to run into each other. It was not only evident that it had been used for many years, but personal notes from its owner were scribbled on its tattered pages.

Ebunoluwa started their session with a prayer asking God to use her as a vessel of His truth. She explained to the princess that her secret to having a successful marriage was having a close relationship with God. That's why she felt it was very important that they start with an explanation of God's original intent for marriage.

"God gave Eve to Adam as a companion or helpmate," she explained. "Their main purpose, according to Genesis 1:28, was to be fruitful and multiply and to care for the garden (their home) and its inhabitants. Even though the meaning of marriage has changed in modern day society, God has not changed His intent."

Zara respectfully nodded her head.

Ebunoluwa went on to patiently explain what a Christian wife looks like using Bathsheba's description in Proverbs 31:10 – 31, which her son, King Solomon, scribed. She shared that Bathsheba was one of King David's wives and the father of her son. Ebunoluwa opened the massive Bible and started to read the instructional text to her starting with verse 10:

"*'A good woman is hard to find, and worth far more than diamonds.'*

When I was a young girl, I was taught that the opinion of others dictated my worth," Iya Ebunoluwa shared. "It wasn't until I became a woman that I realized that I was a valuable commodity and that I determined my worth based on my view of self. What do you see when you look in the mirror, Princess?"

"I am told that I resemble my mother."

"How did they describe her?"

"She was tall, lighter in complexion than me. I have her eyes, and my lips are perfectly shaped like hers."

"I assume they are perfect for Mr. Ezra," Ebunoluwa said. "Is he a good kisser?"

Zara blushed. "Yes, he is a very good kisser. But, keep in mind I don't have anything to compare him to."

Her Iya smiled. "Believe it or not this works to your advantage. It increases your value. You are giving an undefiled gift of self to your intended."

"I have always heard the opposite," Zara said. "That a man wants an experienced woman."

"Perhaps that is true if he only wants a temporary relationship or a one-night stand," Ebunoluwa said with sincerity. "But when a man wants a woman that he can be with forever, her purity is considered a great prize." She paused before asking, "Why do you think your father has gone to great lengths to protect you? He recognizes the value of your virginity."

"I see," Zara thoughtfully responded. Zara also better understood why Sarki was in her bedroom that night. It made her heart ache that a lifetime friend would be capable of such duplicity.

Ebunoluwa took her sullen attitude as apprehension about knowing a man in the biblical sense. She returned to the lesson.

"A woman dictates her own value," Ebunoluwa continued teaching. "She must first be valuable to herself. Then others will soon recognize it in her. That's why boundaries are a good thing. They send the message that your heart is worth the wait."

Zara took a moment to reflect on her Iya's last comment. What a difference between Sarki and E. Sarki wanted to possess her for the kingdom and was willing to use force to obtain it. E., on the other hand, was willing to go to great lengths to win her heart. He was the least likely candidate, yet he willingly paid the higher price for her hand in marriage.

Her Iya continued, "*Her husband trusts her without reserve and never has reason to regret it. Never spiteful, she treats him generously all her life long.*'

"Because a wife values herself, it's easier for her to value others. She always looks for the jewels in her husband and celebrates, respects, and honors him. That's why it's important for parents or the individual to choose well. She was meant to be bound in covenant with this man for life. Do you understand, Princess?"

"Yes, I do. My father chose E. because he felt it was the best choice for me and the kingdom."

"Beeni!" Ebunoluwa continued on to the next verse: "'She shops around for the best *yarns and cottons, and enjoys knitting and sewing.*'

"A wife buys quality goods and products for her family because they deserve the best of what she has to offer them. She relishes her role, and she allows her heart's intent to dictate her actions when caring for her family."

"I can't knit or sew," Zara confessed. "Will you be showing me how to do those things?"

Ebunoluwa reached for her hand. "Oh, Princess," she said, "when this was written thousands of years ago, they lived in an agricultural society. Today we must translate this into what is currently necessary for a wife and mother to do to care for her family. For example, as a royal, your job as a wife and mother would be to make sure that you choose the right kind of staff to provide for your family; those that best reflect how you would want them to be cared for and loved. You would also be required to oversee the process, just like you oversee your kingdom responsibilities. Se o ye o?" her Iya asked to make sure she understood.

"Beeni," Zara said nodding.

"Iyanu," Ebunoluwa said smiling, "let's move on to the next verse. 'She's like a trading ship that sails to faraway places and brings back exotic surprises.'

"She is a pleasant mystery and a gift. You want to continue to make life an adventure, particularly for your husband. A man desires a woman who can speak to his body, mind, and spirit, especially in the different seasons of his life. Always be alert and attentive to what's going on in your family. Your husband may be the head of the family, but you are the actual neck that turns his head. In other words, the admiral may be in charge of the fleet, but you are the captain of the ship. The next scripture reinforces what we discussed earlier."

Ebunoluwa continued reading, "'*She's up before dawn, preparing breakfast for her family and organizing her day.*'

"She is masterful in the art of caring for her family. It is a priority for her, and they know it. They show their appreciation because they are well cared for." Her Iya paused then saying, "Beloved, this may seem like a lot, but God would not have had Bathsheba share this with us if it were an impossible task. We can do all things through Christ Jesus who strengthens us."

Ebunoluwa paused to let the meaning of the last verse linger in the princesses' mind. She wanted Zara to remember that no matter how hard times with her husband and family may get, God would give her strength and sustain her. She looked at Zara, whose smile acknowledged that she clearly understood.

"A Christian wife is also entrepreneurial," her Iya proceeded. "The next scripture states, '*She looks over a field and buys it, then, with money she's put aside, plants a garden*'.

"She is constantly looking for wealth-building opportunities to provide uninterrupted care for her family. Your father has provided well for you, but you are required to continue to build upon his legacy so that there is an inheritance for your children's children.

"Being a wife is a twenty-four hour, seven days a week job. That's why Queen Bathsheba states in the next scripture, '*First thing in the morning, she dresses for work, rolls up her sleeves, eager to get started.*' A wife has a hunger for life, and it's evident in her daily routine. She welcomes the opportunity to be a wife and mother and readily accepts the responsibility and challenges associated with that calling upon her life. '*She senses the worth of her work, is in no hurry to call it quits for the day. She's skilled in the crafts of home and hearth, diligent in homemaking.'* A wife is often a skilled multitasker. As a princess, you already have a sense of what this means. So, make that work to your advantage.

"Princess, I am well aware of your benevolent kindness to your constituents. I have no doubt that you will excel in this next scripture. *'She's quick to assist anyone in need, reaches out to help the poor.* A wife is kind and benevolent toward others and is a role model for her children. Train them up to do likewise. Start at an early age to show them the value of helping others, and when they are ruling the kingdom, they will make this a key part of their political agenda.

"God placed you in this position because He expects to be the center of your marriage. He also expects you to pray instead of worry about any challenges you may face. Here's what the next scripture says about this, *'She doesn't worry about her family when it snows; their winter clothes are all mended and ready to wear. She makes her own clothing, and dresses in colorful linens and silks.'* Remember we are talking about the symbolism here again of how diligent a wife and mother is when caring for her family. She prepares her family for both the good and the challenging times.

"Remember you are the neck that turns the head. In this case you will be the ruler of the kingdom, but your husband should never feel that he is diminished as a result of your role. You should always be supportive of your husband in public forums because his reputation is hindered when you are not. If you have a disagreement, handle it behind closed doors. I have resolved many issues with my husband with pillow talk in the intimacy of our bedroom. Make him feel like he is a king behind closed doors, and in public and he will readily listen when you offer advice or suggestions when you are alone.

"That's the premise for this next scripture that says, *'Her husband is greatly respected when he deliberates with the city fathers.'* Knowledge of your good works will also bring esteem to your husband in high places.

"Again, this next scripture talks about having an entrepreneurial nature, *'She designs gowns and sells them, brings the sweaters she knits to the dress shops. Her clothes are well-made and elegant, and she always faces tomorrow with a smile.'* Because of your position, you will be a role model to other women. Remember, work is pleasurable to a Christian wife, and her positivity encourages others.

"The next scripture says, *'When she speaks, she has something worthwhile to say, and she always says it kindly.'* She is a wise woman who recognizes the power of her tongue.

"Bathsheba had the opportunity to observe the other wives of King David. Her experience and expertise are reflected in these proverbs. She is constantly surveying her family: *'She keeps an eye on everyone in her household, and keeps them all busy and productive.'* A wife manages her household with a finesse that baffles the average human mind. The Master Designer, God, made her that way."

They both laugh.

"Having many wives must have been difficult for King David. I couldn't imagine having numerous husbands," Zara said. "It would be mind boggling for me."

"Well, Beloved," her Iya said, "your father has seen fit that you will marry only one man. I can guarantee you that will be enough. I have had the same husband for over thirty years, and in order to build the kind of marriage that honors God, I've had to be flexible and constantly seek the help of the Holy Spirit, our earthly Divine Helper. When you do that, you will experience the next set of proverbs. *'Her children respect and bless her; her husband joins in with words of praise: 'Many women have done wonderful things, but you've outclassed them all!' Charm can mislead and beauty soon fades. The woman to be admired and praised is the woman who lives in the Fear-of-God.'*

"When a family praises the woman of the house, it's a good sign that they are content and fulfilled. A wife becomes a Proverbs 31 woman when she reverences her God. She recognizes that He is the source of her success, and those in heaven and earth will declare, '*Give her everything she deserves! Adorn her life with praises!*' Hallelujah!"

Ebunoluwa closed her Bible saying, "Well that's enough for today. Your homework is to write your own description of a Proverbs 31 woman for us to discuss during tomorrow's session. Also bring any questions you may have about what I've covered today."

"Absolutely Iya," Zara said. "May I make an observation?"

"Yes."

"I don't see how a queen can run a household and a kingdom at the same time."

"Princess, you have an advantage that other women don't have."

"What's that?"

"You are already practicing most of these principles as a royal. You are beautiful, wise, protective, and kind. Your people love and adore you and sing your praises throughout the dynasty. You face each new task without complaining with a smile. Regardless of what's going on in your life, you embrace each day like it's full of new opportunities. I believe marriage and children will be an asset to your reign."

"I sure hope so."

After a delicious dinner of Jollof Rice, fried plantains, and Ponmo, the young princess went to her bedroom to complete her homework assignment. Zara took an academic approach to her task. Meanwhile, God was working in her heart. She initially studied Proverbs 31:10 – 31 in multiple versions of the Bible on the Bible App to gain a broader understanding of the writer's intent. Then she outlined the key points identified by her Iya and made a companion list of her own thoughts about each one.

She looked up at the clock, and it was close to midnight. She decided that this princess needed her beauty sleep. She traded her sweats for a candy cane striped cotton night shirt. After lazily pumping up her pillows, she laid her weary head down and went to sleep immediately. Her dreams were of a certain handsome blue-eyed man who adored her as he attempted to unwrapped the mystery of the woman that was to become his bride.

Her heart smiled at that revelation in the morning. As she was gathering the pearls of her dreams, her cell phone rang. A picture of the object of her dreams appeared, and her heart rejoiced again.

Zara's betrothed was also preparing for six weeks of military training in preparation for his role as Prince. This would all take place at Camp Lemonnier Dijbouti, the only U.S. military base in Africa. The twelve-month program had been condensed to accommodate Oba Jaiye's request. Ezra Jr. was expected to be able to protect the kingdom and his family. His abbreviated program consisted of Combat and Recreational Physical Training, Hand-to-Hand Combat, Taekwondo, Rifle and Pistol Shooting Exercises, Land and Water Obstacle Courses, Fieldcraft, Map Reading and Hand Grenade Throwing. When he saw the training agenda, he almost passed out. The only comfort was that he would be surrounded by fellow Americans who could empathize with his challenges of adapting in a foreign land. The king assured him that he was confident of his successful completion. After all, the prize was a lot bigger than the pain he would endure over the next month and a half.

Zara and Ebunoluwa decided to meet in her study for their remaining sessions. On the previous evening Zara crafted a summary to share with her Iya of what she learned from the previous Bridal Bootcamp session on the Proverbs 31 Woman from the scriptures written by Queen Bathsheba. It looked like the following:

> *The characteristics of a Proverbs 31 wife and mother include her virtue, her value and her trustworthiness. Strength and dignity are also characteristic of this woman. She does good and shuns evil. She is industrious, an entrepreneur, and a provider. Her family is one of the highest priorities in her life. She is kind and generous to others. She is a strong woman that accepts the challenges that come with the monumental task of serving as a godly wife and mother. Leaving a legacy and making provisions for her children's children is also very important to her.*

"Great job Princess! The Proverbs 31 wife is virtuous and she loves God!" Ebunoluwa exclaimed. "There were many women in the Bible who were full of virtue and faith. Their passion for God was fueled by their love for Him. A prime example was Ruth. She was a Moabite woman who fell in love with a Hebrew man who relocated to Moab after there was a famine in his homeland with his family. Unfortunately, her husband died before they were able to conceive a child, and she was widowed at an early age. This was also the fate of her mother-in-law and her sister-in-law. Her mother-in-law, Naomi decided to return to her homeland. She encouraged her daughters-in-law to do the same and to return to their families. Orpah decided to follow her advice, but Ruth choose to follow Naomi.Listen to their conversation as I read Ruth 1:8 -22."

'Then Orpah kissed Naomi goodbye, but Ruth hugged her and stayed. Naomi said, 'Look, your sister-in-law has gone back to her own people and her own gods. You should do the same.' But Ruth said, '"Don't force me to leave you! Don't force me to go back to my own people. Let me go with you. Wherever you go, I will go. Wherever you sleep, I will sleep. Your people will be my people. Your God will be my God. Where you die, I will die, and that is where I will be buried. I ask the LORD to punish me if I don't keep this promise: Only death will separate us.'

"Naomi had touched Ruth's life to the point that death could not separate her from her. She honored her departed husband by standing by the elderly woman and caring for her in her old age. She had high moral standards that prompted her to make the ultimate act of love: sacrifice. She was willing to walk away from everything—her family, her country, and her religion."

"Naomi eventually relented, and Ruth followed her back to Bethlehem where she found a job gleaning in the wheat field to provide food for their table. There she met a man named Boaz, the owner of the field, and she fell in love with him. Naomi instructed her on how to win his heart, and he went through the arduous process of becoming their *kinsmen redeemer* .They were soon married, and she bore a son and they named him Obed. He was the father of Jesse who was the father of David, who was a direct descendant of Jesus Christ."

"The moral of this story is that her character spoke volumes not only to the people she loved but also to those who observed how she loved others, so much so, that their praises got back to one of the richest men in their city who was highly respected by the elders at the city gates, Boaz."

"It is imperative that you live a virtuous life, honoring God, your family, and your country. You must become a role model for the women in your kingdom by honoring your husband by living a life in private and public that exemplifies high moral standards. Often sometimes making uncomfortable sacrifices by doing so, but knowing that God sees your good works and will honor you and your family because of them."

Zara sat back and pondered the words of her Iya. She was mystified by the story because, it was so close to E.'s story. He was making the ultimate sacrifice to be with her. Leaving all things behind to build a lifelong relationship with her and the family that is yet to come.

She asked, "Can a man be virtuous?"

Ebunoluwa laughed, "Of course he can, but our focus is on how one becomes a virtuous wife. Are you missing your beloved, Princess?"

"I guess I am. Iya, why does my heart feel so empty without him?"

She smiled saying, "Princess, because it now beats for him."

"He should be back to the palace compound for a visit soon, shouldn't he?"

"Yes. He said Father has promised that he can return for a brief visit next month when his baba comes for a visit."

"Well, we should be through with your training by then. So. You will be able to spend all the time you want with him."

"Thank you, Iya, I don't know what I would do without your cheerful counsel. Ever since Victoria has been forbidden to come to the palace, I've been without a confidante."

"You are so welcomed my dear princess. Now let's move on to the next topic: A virtuous wife is valuable to her husband and her children."

Ebunoluwa went on to describe the lives of two influential queens, Helen of Troy and Queen Esther. She started their conversation by describing Helen of Troy, the daughter of Zeus and Leda, who was considered the most beautiful woman in the world. The Trojan prince, Paris, stole her from her husband Menelaus, the king of Sparta. Menelaus convinced his brother to go to war with him to recapture his wife and was successful in his pursuit. Unfortunately, she became the poster child for moral degradation and lust as a result of her beauty and is often known as having "the face that launched a thousand ships." Helen was valuable because of her beauty and had many suitors, but she lacked integrity and a moral core.

On the other hand, Ebunoluwa described Queen Esther as an old-testament queen who loved her God and His people. "Her virtue won the heart of King Ahasuerus when he was in pursuit of a wife," Ebunoluwa said. "She stood out among hundreds of women because of her beauty, confidence, and intellect. When the other women were relying on their external appearance to win the heart of the king, she relied on her ability to speak to his heart. She gained favor with the eunuch in charge, and he instructed her on how to gain favor with the king."

"Esther was merely an orphan in her cousin's house when she was carried off to the king's palace. After he chose her as his queen, it was made evident that the Jews had an enemy called Haman who was a chief counselor in the palace. He devised a clever scheme to kill all of the Jews throughout the land, and actually sent out decrees with the king's signet seal on them signifying their validity. Mordecai, her cousin, sent Queen Esther a message about their impending destruction, and she approached her husband to appeal for her people."

Ebunoluwa turned the page of the Bible and began reading,

> 'On the third day Esther put on her royal robes and stood in the inner court of the palace, in front of the king's hall. The king was sitting on his royal throne in the hall, facing the entrance. When he saw Queen Esther standing in the court, he was pleased with her and held out to her the gold scepter that was in his hand. So, Esther approached and touched the tip of the scepter.

> *'Then the king asked, '"What is it, Queen Esther? What is your request? Even up to half the kingdom, it will be given you.' (Esther 5:1 -3 NIV)*

"Making an appeal to her husband, the king, could have cost her her life because she had not received an invitation from him," Ebunoluwa explained. "But he spared her and her people after hearing about Haman's plot and learning the true ethnicity of his wife. She was valuable because God could trust her obedience to implement his rescue plan for his people from their enemies.

"Princess, when you are queen, you can be an asset to your God, your husband and your family, and your people if you seek God's heavenly counsel and counselors. But it's your choice," she said then paused. "God gives us free will because He wants us to serve Him out of the love we have for Him. Esther loved her God more than she loved her own life.

"Your homework today is to create a list of the things you love and why you love them. Then, Princess Zara, I would have you prioritize them based on your perceived importance, and we will discuss your list first thing in the morning. Do you have any questions about this assignment?"

"No. Perhaps tomorrow," Zara replied. "I would like to do some additional studying on both of these queens; they are very intriguing."

"Yes, they are," Ebunoluwa agreed. "Well, have a nice day."

"You too, Ebunoluwa."

The next day was dark and cloudy, it was as if the sun forgot how to shine. It may have been a dreary day outside of the palace walls, but inside the servants buzzed around like busy bees because the king would soon be returning. Whenever the king was on an extended trip away from the palace, the matter was always of the utmost importance and often secretive.

It was rumored that he annually made several trips over the years to the bush searching for a powerful witch doctor to reverse the curse put on his life by Zara's grandmother. It had been over twenty years, and he refused to accept the fact that he could not produce a male heir.

Recently, he heard of a small distant village where every woman over the age of fourteen had initially given birth to a male child. He decided to secretly spend a two-week holiday in a beach house not too far from the village. It was his desire to impregnate one of the women in a last attempt to produce a male heir. The local village chief had provided three viable candidates for a handsome price. By the time he was ready to retire, the child would be of age, and he would have trained him to be a good king.

He chuckled. "Fate would not have the final say in the future of my kingdom," he thought. After all, he was king, and he could do whatever he wanted.

Zara wrestled with her assignment. Her natural inclination was to put the kingdom before anything else on the list, but it just didn't seem right. There were so many more new variables in her life to consider. Her upcoming marriage was now at the top of the list. She almost yearned for her good old college days, when life was much simpler.

She wished she could talk to her father about this quandary, but that was just a pipe dream. He was always too busy to have an extended conversation with her, and Vincent was swamped with his added responsibilities of being the kingdom's new security director. Then there was Sarki's disappearance; he was still a fugitive. She knew what her father would do to him, once he found him. It was just a matter of time before he was located. Pondering the ultimate demise of a close friend didn't bode well with Zara. It made her look closely at her own mortality.

Was there anything else besides the kingdom life she had known all of her twenty-one years? Yes, she'd visited other countries, but nothing compared to home. But what if home did not exist? What if her father, for some reason lost his throne? What would happen to her? It was customary for warring nations to kill the king's entire family when they took control of a nation. It chilled her to think of her death on those terms. She was a mere mortal living in a world that was full of uncertainty; everything it was built on was as fragile as the thread that was unraveling in her linen shirt.

At that moment Zara realized that just as she had a definite beginning, there was a definite ending pending. She'd seen death on numerous occasions, but it had never been as close to her as Sarki's imminent demise. What would happen to his okan when he breathed his last breath? Where would he spend eternity? What would his lehin iku experience be? Before the attempted rape, she had known him to be a faithful and loyal friend. But, as head of her father's security, he'd been required to do things that ensured the kingdom's safety, and that included killing anyone who had opposed the king or his kingdom in any way.

Suddenly she was angry with herself. She had purposefully ignored what was going on around her. If her head wasn't in the books, it was filled with schoolgirl dreams. No wonder E.'s mother had challenged her ability to be a good wife to her son. She was still acting like an omo. In a way, her father had crippled her by sheltering her from the real world. He thought he was protecting her, but in a lot of ways he had hindered her passage into womanhood.

The world was cruel, and bad people and good people often did bad things in it that hurt others. She would be queen one day, following in the footsteps of her father. Would she rule as he did? Would she actually have someone killed if it benefited the kingdom? This realization caused her to weep. She knew that if she decided to do so her complicity whether directly or indirectly made her as responsible as those who actually did the dirty work. Who was she to take someone's life away?

"No!" she screamed.

But her father's blood ran through her veins. She was capable of doing what he did and so much more because of her ignorance. He had trained her all of these years to be a female version of himself. How could she escape this relentless hold he and the kingdom had on her? It wasn't being a royal that challenged her. It was being a killer, destroying families, and being a god to her people that would ultimately destroy her. She could not make the kingdom her top priority. She would not! There had to be another way. She would seek the counsel of her Iya immediately.

Zara found her Iya in her office awaiting their meeting. She was sitting in her favorite chair reading her Bible, a book that seemed to be attached to her wrist. The princess was acutely aware of her strong faith, but wondered about her antiquated beliefs. The idea of someone coming from a celestial heaven to earth to save all of mankind was a bit unrealistic. But Ebunoluwa had a made up mind, and who was she to challenge her. She had bigger problems that she needed to address before she was put in a position that would have been impossible to change. Iya was the wisest woman she knew, her monotheistic views excluded. She pondered her approach. She came to the conclusion that honesty would be her best course of action.

"Good morning Ebunoluwa," Zara said softly to announce her presence. "How was your evening?"

"Good morning, Princess Zara," Ebunoluwa responded. "My dreams were pleasant, and my night restful. And yours?"

"Not quite as good as yours I am afraid. I had some problems with my assignment."

"Really? How can I help, Beloved?"

"I wrestled with my commitment as a queen. With all the new changes in my life, I'm not sure I can handle everything that goes along with being a royal. If I'm to be a wife, and a mother someday, how will this influence my role as a leader of this great nation?"

"Princess Zara, you can't do it."

"What?"

"You can't handle everything that you have been purposed to do on your own."

"Iya, you've lost confidence in my abilities?" Zara asked with disappointment. "Then why are you here?"

"I am here because God sent me here to help you," Ebunoluwa patiently answered.

"But you just said I can't do this on my own."

"Yes, I did. I can't either. The truth is that none of us can. We all need God's help to fulfill our purpose in life."

"Which god, Iya?" Zara asked. "Tell me which one, and I will personally go to the Holy Hill and pay homage to it. Because life has suddenly gotten more complicated than I imagined."

"You don't need to go to the Holy Hill or anywhere else." Ebunoluwa placed her hand over Zara's heart saying, "He's right here, Beloved."

"I've never known that a God can reside in a human being."

"Why not? After all He made us. If a monkey gets pregnant, what do we expect to see it give birth too? A baby monkey, correct?"

"Yes, but there are so many gods, each with its own purpose. It's hard to know which one is the most dominant one."

"Princess, those gods that you are talking about were created in the imaginations of man."

"No, Ebunoluwa," Zara said, "I have seen their power..."

"No," Ebunoluwa interrupted, "what you saw was the power of *Oya*. He is a master manipulator and deceiver. He can only mimic what the Master has created."

"So, what are you saying Iya? A whole continent of people can't be wrong in what they believe."

"People often believe what they want to believe, whether it is truth or a lie. They do so to suit their purpose. There is only one God, Zara, and He created man out of the dust of the earth. He literally breathed life into clay, and man became a living being. He created man in His image. When you look into the mirror, you are looking back at Him."

"God looks like me?" Zara asked pointing at herself.

Ebunoluwa smiled and said, "No, Beloved, you look like Him. There's a difference. The Good Book says that He knew us before we were formed in our mother's womb. Meaning, He imagined us, and we were created. Just like an inventor envisions his creation before he develops a blueprint or a seamstress sees her design in her mind before she actually cuts out a pattern to create it."

"I see. Well, why isn't this God well known in our dynasty?"

"Many people know of him. You father has designated the dynasty a Christian nation, but he did it for political reasons, not personal. He has mixed in some of the Christian rituals with our tribal customs to appease the people. For example, your betrothal ceremony. I digress, please forgive me. Let me answer your original question. The people in our dynasty do not have an intimate relationship with God because they have not received his son as their Lord and Savior. In order to know the Father, you must go through His son, Jesus Christ."

"I've heard of Jesus before, but no one has ever explained to me that I needed to believe in him in order to get to God. Why is that so?"

"We all are sinners in need of a savior. We have a natural inclination to sin because we were born into a fallen world. Are you familiar with Adam and Eve?"

"Yes. They are the original father and mother of all humankind."

"Yes, but they sinned in the Garden of Eden, and their consequences are our consequences because all of mankind are the fruit of the loins of our original parents. We all have a sinful nature that rules within each of us. Jesus came to set us free from our sins and to give us eternal life."

"Why did God design such an elaborate plan? It seems that if He created us, He should have been able to reprogram us for good, not evil."

"That may seem like a viable solution, but unfortunately it wasn't that easy. Adam and Eve both chose their fate. Because of their actions, we must also make a choice. Their disobedience interrupted God's plan for us to walk in total dependence on Him and to reap the benefits of being his children."

"Eden was a place of euphoria. There was no sickness or disease. Man was in charge of the animals and the land, and everything lived in harmony. When *Oya* tempted the woman, she made an unfortunate choice based on the half-truths he told her. She trusted him without any evidence that he was trustworthy."

"So why should I trust this God?"

"Beloved, ask him yourself," Ebunoluwa emphatically declared. "He will answer you."

"Why would the God of the universe answer me?"

"Because he loves you and when you love someone, you trust them. He trusts that in your asking the question, that you genuinely believe that he has the answer because of his divinity. Any more questions?"

"No. You've given me a lot to think about."

"Good. This conversation has been a great introduction to our topic today: A virtuous woman is trustworthy."

"Wait a minute, I do have another question. Should I go somewhere special to ask God about why I should trust Him?"

"No, he can speak to you anywhere."

"How will I know its Him and not some other deity?"

"Your heart will bear witness to his answer," Ebunoluwa said. "Now let's look at another interesting woman from the Bible. She was an unlikely candidate for God's attention, but her curiosity opened her heart to the possibility of a relationship with Him. Her name is Rahab, a Canaanite, and she was a prostitute."

"Really?"

"Yes, really."

"There is no clear evidence as to how she made the choice to do this line of work, but she was well known and lived in a wall that protected the city of Jericho. Before the Israelites came across the Jordan into their promised land, their leader, Joshua, sent two spies to scout out the city. Unfortunately, they were discovered, and Rahab hid them and helped them escape. They left her with a promise: because of her actions, she and her household would be saved from the destruction of Jericho, and she would become a part of the people of Israel."

"Why would He give such a gift to a common prostitute?"

"It's simple. He had her heart. He could trust her to do the right thing. The all-knowing God knew her before she was conceived in her mother's womb and saw that her heart was pliable. She may not have chosen her lifestyle. Her family may have come on hard times, and she would have been sold so that they could live. According to her cultural norms, she would have been considered unacceptable as a prospective wife. But God saw her worthiness and created an opportunity for her to be saved, even her whole family was rescued as a result of her actions. She eventually ended up marrying into the bloodline of Jesus Christ. The Bible says,

> *'In the same way, was not even Rahab the prostitute considered righteous for what she did when she gave lodging to the spies and sent them off in a different direction?' (James 2:25 NIV)*

"God saw her potential and rewarded her for her belief in Him and obedience in a land where she was a minority. He trusted her to help bring about His promise to His people. He knew what she was made of because he designed her. Regardless of what life had dealt her before that moment, when it really counted, she came through for Him. She was trustworthy. Her occupation had little to do with her decision to obey God. Her heart knew the value of obedience to the Israelites God."

"How can she be a prostitute, and her heart not be corrupted?"

"Princess, we all are born with a corrupt heart, but God has the power to change a surrendered heart to perform His will. The Bible says that He can even turn the heart of kings."

"Kini eyi? What manner of God is this?"

"He is the one and only Sovereign God. He is mighty in strength and power, and He loves you my dear princess."

"Are you sure?"

"Yes, I am."

Ebunoluwa grasped her hand. "Let's pray my dear." The young princess nodded her agreement. With both of their heads bowed, Ebunoluwa prayed:

Father God,

My dear Zara is seeking you and your truth. May she find You. My belief is that she will know You and the voice of a stranger she will not follow, in the name of Jesus, Amen."

Ebunoluwa released the young woman's hand, saying, "Your homework is to study the life of Rahab and to talk with God. I brought a gift for you today." She reached into her tote bag and handed her a copy of the Beautiful Word Bible with her name engraved on the cover. "Use this in your studies."

"Thank you, Iya," Zara acknowledged the gift and placed it on the desk. "You've given me a lot to think about today."

"That's why I am here. Feel free to reach out to me if you have any additional questions. I am available to you at any time."

"Thank you, again for the insightful meeting."

"You are very welcomed Beloved."

Both women left the room with a lot on their minds. Zara contemplating her future as queen, and Ebunoluwa, contemplating the young woman's salvation.

Periodically the princess would meet with the chaperones for dinner to get caught up on their activities and to hear about their antics with Vincent. In the absence of the king's security guards, the Alagbatas were now assigned palace guard duty. So, they not only had their ears to the wall about what was happening in the palace, but they were also filled with the palace gossip.

That evening they were dining on Jollof Rice, chicken, and steamed vegetables with a complimentary exotic fruit tray for dessert in her suite's dining area. Most of her chaperones were at least six feet, tall so their long legs were battling for room under the small dining room table. It was a matter of teasing by the princess who was a relentless oppressor. Once she got the official security report from her chaperones, she was beguiled with tales of palace escapades. Their conversation drifted to powerful African women after a brief discussion of how the palace chef had extraordinary control over every kingdom official because she was a master at preparing multiple memorable cuisines. They were all hooked like addicts on meth to her cooking.

Zara began to question the Alagbatas about their knowledge of royals, particularly women kings. The conversation drifted to the infamous Queen (*Sarauniya*) Amina of Zaria, the West African warrior queen. She was the first woman to become a female ruler in a male-dominated society. Her efforts as the ruler of the Hausa people expanded their territory to its largest borders in the history of North

Africa. It was a mecca for trade and commerce. The princess jokingly expressed her desire to be just like Queen Amina when she took over her father's throne.

The room suddenly got eerily quiet. Each of the chaperones lowered their heads. The princess was surprised at their unusual response to her declaration. She queried each woman about the feasibility of her statement, and there was again complete silence. An agitated Zara finally demanded an answer. Each of the women turned to Nafisa to respond. The otherwise fearless warrior hesitantly stood and faced her royal highness. She was well aware that this gentle dove was the daughter of a fierce lion who would have no problem tearing her head off if she disobeyed her.

"Your Highness," Nafisa said slowly, "it would grieve us greatly to dishonor you."

"How would you dishonor me if we were just kidding?" Zara asked. "Queen Amina was an asset to our people. Are you implying that I shouldn't want to be like her?"

Nafisa looked down before she answered, "No, My Highness."

"So, what is the problem?"

Nafisa looked up at her fellow warriors, and she received a nod from Hiba. "Princess Zara, Queen Amina was also a human being. Yes, she did great things for our beloved continent as a leader, but war does strange things to a woman if she hasn't found a way to balance her femininity with her power."

"So, what aren't you saying?"

"It is rumored that Queen Amina refused to marry and sought her pleasure with a temporary bridegroom in every town that she went through."

"What's wrong with that? It's not my desired course of action, but is this not uncommon behavior for male warriors. Why should it be any different for her?"

Silence.

"I asked a question Nafisa," Zara demanded. "I expect an answer."

Hiba nodded again.

"Your Highness, Queen Amina not only bedded the men, but she beheaded them the next morning so that they could not share what happened the night before in her bed."

"She what?"

"She killed her lovers."

"My God!"

The uncomfortable silence returned. Somewhere in the moments that elapsed, Nafisa found the courage to ask a question. "Princess Zara, may we be released to our rooms?"

"Yes. Our evening together is done. Good night."

This release was followed with a chorus of good nights from the Alagbatas. As the ladies made haste to their rooms, Nafisa thanked Hiba for her much-welcomed support during the difficult conversation. They all wondered what their future would be like if the king heard about this troublesome conversation. They all slept with their spears close to their beds that night.

Ebunoluwa spent the night on her knees petitioning Heaven for the soul of her protege. When she drifted by the dining area, Zara was having a delightful conversation with the Alagbatas. It amused her to see the princess having fun with a group of her peers. The young woman deserved every moment of happiness she was gifted. So, when the princess came storming into their early morning meeting, she was shocked. It was obvious that Zara was troubled by something. She said a quick prayer for guidance and approached the princess with caution.

"E kaaro," Princess Zara.

"E kaaro," Ebunoluwa. "Unfortunately, I did not get to complete my homework. Perhaps we will need to postpone today's session."

"No, Beloved. We will continue as planned. The homework is for your enrichment and to better facilitate your learning experience."

"But..."

"My dear princess, this isn't primary school. When you find the time to complete your assignment, I will be ready to review it and help you in any way that I can. Let's proceed as planned unless there is something that you would like to discuss before we begin today."

Silence.

"Princess Zara?"

"Are you familiar with the infamous Queen Amina?"

"Yes, I am. She was a great leader, and her people loved her because she brought wealth and prosperity to Hausa. Your father reminds me of her. Why?"

"Did you know about the rumored fate of her many lovers?"

Zara blushed and glared at her Iya. Ebunoluwa wrinkled her forehead trying to recollect what Zara could possibly be referring to. Then it hit her, and she began to rock back and forth in belly busting laughter. Once she regained her composure, she questioned Zara.

"Is that what's bothering you, Beloved?"

"What's so funny? It's horrible that a queen would carry on like that, especially when the world is watching."

Ebunoluwa moved to sit on the comfortable settee beside the princess and placed her arm around her. "Zara, there are many things that our ancestors did that we would now consider deplorable, but we must learn from their mistakes, not replicate them."

"You mentioned during the last session that we all had a sin nature. I am terrified by the possibility of my turning out like her."

"You won't. You come from a different seed."

"How can you say that? My father is cut from the same cloth that she is; you said so yourself."

"No, Beloved, you must take the good from both of them and throw away the bad."

"How can I do that? They weren't able to do it."

"They didn't want to, Beloved. With God's help you can and will be greater than them. You must make that choice though."

"Which God are you talking about Iya?"

"The I AM that I AM!" Ebunoluwa said confidently. "God told Moses in the book of Genesis to refer to Him as the I AM when they asked who sent him to be a leader to his people. Zara you have asked a legitimate question, but there is only one true God. I believe once you ask Him your question, He will show you who He is and why you should trust Him."

"Let's move on to today's lesson. It's such a coincidence that we started the day talking about royals, because we are going to take a detour and look at a woman in the Bible who handled her assignment quite differently, her name is Jezebel. She was the daughter of the ruler of the Phoenician cities of Tyre and Sidon, priest-king Ethbaal. She married King Ahab of Israel."

Ebunoluwa reached for her Bible. She began reading, "In 1 Kings 16:30-33 it says,

> *'Ahab son of Omri did more evil in the eyes of the Lord than any of those before him. He not only considered it trivial to commit the sins of Jeroboam son of Nebat, but he also married Jezebel daughter of Ethbaal king of the Sidonians, and began to serve Baal and worship him. He set up an altar for Baal in the temple of Baal that he built in Samaria. Ahab also made an Asherah pole and did more to arouse the anger of the Lord, the God of Israel, than did all the kings of Israel before him.'*

"She not only introduced pagan worship to God's people, but she also killed his prophets and manipulated his people for her and her husband's selfish whims. Her life ended with an appropriate epithet to her scandalous reign. She was thrown from a window, trampled by a horse, and eaten by dogs after falling from a tower."

"Princess Zara, Queen Jezebel was ruled by her lust for power. Your precious DNA isn't remotely like hers. Being a royal doesn't define who you are; it doesn't even define what you do. You do. If you want to do a good job, you go to your Creator and ask Him what's the best way to do that in the world He created."

Zara uncharacteristically fell into her Iya's arms and started to pout.

"This is too hard Iya! I don't know that I can do this."

"God will help you my child. Trust him."

She held Zara there for a long time speaking comforting words in her ears. Those words eventually turned into prayers, and they finished the day's session with the princess fast asleep in the arms of her earthly comforter.

Vincent found them there several hours later. He gently lifted the princess into his arms, carried her to her room, laid her down, and tucked her in for the night. Around 11:00 p.m. Zara's cellphone rang. She was startled by Michael Bublé's *I Can't Help Falling in Love*, which was lovingly assigned to E. She fumbled for a second with the authentication.

"Zara?" E. whispered.

"I can barely hear you," she said. "Can you speak up?"

"No. Can you put your telephone on speaker?"

She pressed speaker on her phone, then asked him, "Is everything alright?"

"Yes and no. Your father runs a strict camp. I had to get my body guards interested in a soccer game in order to sneak away and give you a call."

"You're up this late?"

"Yes. Zara, I'm sorry to interrupt your sleep, but I just had to speak to you. I really miss our prenuptial adventures."

"I miss you too. Actually, I am glad you called. I had a rough day."

"Really, you?"

"Yes me. I'm human, silly."

"A very beautiful one with mocha velvety skin and deep brown eyes that I love to get lost in."

"That was sweet, but I'm serious."

"Okay. Well, what's the problem? There might not be much I can do from here, but I will try."

"Well, I am wrestling with how I am going to handle my kingdom responsibilities, marriage and raising a family."

"Interesting. You know that you already have all the help you need, especially from me. That's what marriage is about. Isn't that what you are learning with your Iya—how to do all of that?"

"Yes, that's what's prompting all of these questions."

"Wow, it must be working."

"Unfortunately, it's working too well."

"Don't you want to be able to rock this thing called marriage. I know I do. That's why I am going through this grueling bootcamp that your Dad designed."

"Is it really hard?"

"For a white boy from the good ole USA, yes. But you're worth it. So, what's really going on?"

"Please don't think badly of us, but some of my ancestors were murderers. Their excuse was that it was necessary for the kingdom. I don't want to rule Dala Dynasty that way if I am ever in that position."

"Then don't do it."

"It's not that simple."

"Why is that?"

"I haven't figured it out yet."

"I see. So, what does your Iya say about all of this?"

"She says that we all have a fallen nature, and the only way we can do good is to have a relationship with God through his son, Jesus Christ."

"She's right."

"Why do you say that?"

"Because my life didn't turn around until I made that very same decision."

"You never shared that with me before."

"Well, it hasn't been easy to spend a lot of time with you lately."

"True."

"Don't worry, my beloved princess, I will be home soon, and we will make it a priority to have this discussion then, but I must go before they come looking for me. These fellas have a short attention span. I really don't want to leave you, especially now. But know that I will be praying for you continuously and thinking about you every free second that I can."

"Well, you've given me a lot to think about. Come back as soon as you can."

"I will. I promise." E. blew her a brief kiss and hung up.

Zara sighed and laid back down until she realized that she still had yesterday's clothes on. She remedied the situation quickly and returned to her comfortable pillows and covers hoping to dream of her beloved. Before she closed her eyes, she allowed her heart to ask God the million-dollar question of the day, *"Why should I trust You?"* Immediately, He dispatched a host of angels led by the warrior Archangel Gabriel with an answer.

Radiating beams of sunshine kissed the garden bench greeting Ebunoluwa as she sat down to study her Bible and pray before her session with Zara. It was their last session, and she had mixed emotions about it coming to an end. The hypnotic sent of the Irises couldn't even distract her. Her inner sadness was peppered with regret for not accomplishing what she thought God had sent her to the palace to do; share His love with the princess.

Today she would share the story of one of the Bible's noblest woman warriors, Deborah. She sensed that Zara was experiencing doubt about her rule as a queen because of the injustice and unrighteousness that had previously prevailed in her land. Some kind of way, she had to convince her that with God on her side, she would become the queen her people needed.

Ebunoluwa prayed:

> *Father, please help me to minister Your love to this princess. You have called her to reign in righteousness, and our people need to know your true compassion and love like no other time in our history. You have called her for such a time as this. Use me in whatever way you deem necessary to fulfill Your will. I am yours, you are the potter and I am the clay. In Jesus' name I pray, Amen.*

As she raised her head, she could see the princess approaching. It was a beautiful day, and it seemed as though the garden was beckoning them to sit for a while and enjoy its beauty. As Zara got closer, Ebunoluwa stood and greeted her with a smile.

"Good morning, Princess. You look rejuvenated."

"I am. Thank you, Iya. And thank you for yesterday," she said embracing Ebunoluwa.

"Your kindness was so healing. Your children are fortunate to have you as their mother."

"Thank you, Princess. That's a true compliment coming from you."

They sat down on the bench.

"I assume we will have our lesson out here today?" Zara said.

"If it pleases you, my dear princess, of course we can."

"What's the lesson for today?"

"In our final lesson, we will look at the prophetess, Deborah in Judges 4 and 5. Deborah was a true woman of valor. She was the only female judge in Israel during the time when the people were falling away from God. In her role as a prophetess, she expressed the will of God through divine revelation. As a judge, she ensured that the Israelites were living as God had commanded them. She sat under the Palm of Deborah and settled the disputes of her people. She was respected and trusted because it was evident that she had been sent by God. Her righteous leadership gained her the love of the people in a male-dominated society."

"One day she sent for Barak, the son of Abinoam to share with him a word from the Lord, the God of Israel. God commanded Barak to take ten thousand men up to Mount Tabor to fight Sisera, the commander of Jabin's army, and God promised him victory."

"Barak petitioned the judge to go with him to the battle and threatened not to go if she didn't. He was confident in her ability as a representative of God to ensure his win. She went, and the glory of that victory went to her. But she wasn't the only woman that contributed to Israel's victory that day."

"Sisera escaped on foot during the course of the battle, and he ran to the tent of Jael, the wife of Heber, who had an alliance between King Jabin and Heber's family. Jael invited Sisera in for refreshments. When he fell asleep, Jael took a hammer and put a tent peg into his temple.

The Israelites later fought against King Jabin and utterly destroyed his kingdom. Afterward, Israel had peace for forty years. As a tribute to their victory, Deborah and Barak sang a song of praise to God."

Ebunoluwa shared her Bible with the Princess. The birds decided to chirp a happy symphony as they both reviewed Judges 4 and 5. The princess was astonished by what she read. Deborah was a leader like her, and she got her instructions directly from God. How amazing was that? All of her life, Zara had gotten her instructions from her father, her instructors, and her caregivers, but this woman, Deborah, had a direct line to God, and He helped her rule His people. Her Iya had answered one of Zara's greatest fears by sharing the prophetess with her. This God would even go into battle with you and give you a winning military strategy to defeat your enemies. She wanted to verify her thoughts, so she questioned her Iya.

"So, Deborah was a leader?"

"Yes, God commissioned her to lead His people in a time when they needed guidance."

"This God actually commissions people to be leaders?"

"Yes, the one and only true God empowers leaders to perform His righteous will on the earth."

"I see. And He is more powerful than any other God?"

"He is Elohim. This name reflects his sovereignty and absolute power. He is also called by other names such as El Shaddai, Adonai, Abba, and El Elyon. They all point to His divinity and power over and in the earthly realm and beyond."

"I see. I want to know this God. How can we make it happen today?"

Vincent peered out of the window in the conference room above the garden. It was in full bloom today. Whenever he needed a moment to think, he found the nearest window to remind him of the beauty of God's creation and His meticulous care when designing it and its beauty. To his surprise, in the garden below, he saw the princess and Ebunoluwa sitting on a bench in intimate prayer. Her Iya was holding Zara's hand, and they both had bent heads petitioning the God of the universe. He felt an unspeakable sense of joy. God was answering the prayers of Vincent and his darling wife at that very moment, and he rejoiced.

CHAPTER 07

$\mathcal{Z}$ara missed the quiet of the palace compound. She was just getting used to studying her new Bible and spending time with God when her whole world turned upside down because the king was arriving. Everyone was in a frenzy, especially the security detail that was in pursuit of Sarki. There was still no news of his location, and they knew that the king would be livid.

He was expected earlier in the week and was delayed because of a civil matter that required his attention in one of the outlying villages. E.'s father was also arriving today. The king wanted to be at the palace when that happened, but his delay was unavoidable, so Zara was assigned to greet Ezra at the airport. This involved extra security. Three vehicles accommodated all of the chaperones, the princess, and their American guest. Two of the chaperones rode in her vehicle while the others were in the vehicle before and after her SUV in the caravan to the private airfield. The three black Range Rovers were a sight to behold after being out of commission for over a month.

The drive to the airport was a little over an hour. Zara had plenty of time to think about her sessions with Ebunoluwa. Something miraculous had happened in her life. Daily she was learning more and more about the women in the Bible, and how God used them in their humanity to perform supernatural things. She now understood her mission wasn't about her ability. It was about her submission to God, her calling, and her husband when she married. She loved the fact that the Bible shared the good and the bad of the lives of the children of Israel. It wasn't a public relations effort to project a certain image or build a particular brand. Men had tried to use it for their own personal means, but the will of God always prevailed. She marveled at how a book written so many years ago could stand the test of time. Its modern day relevance was astonishing.

As they neared the airport, Zara's musings came to an end. It was now time for her to greet her future father-in-law. She missed his son a lot, but he would do as a pleasant substitute for a while.

After the military training, Ezra Jr. was assigned another week on the road. This training consisted of a pilgrimage to the dynasty's most influential cities. The purpose of this trip was to get to know the customs and people of the Dala Dynasty. He was acutely aware that he stood out where ever he went, but not once did he feel unwelcomed, even in the bush. As a matter of fact, they went to great lengths to make him feel at home.

They were finally on the road back to the dynasty palace compound, back to his betrothed. He imagined that she would be glad to see him, at least that's what she shared with him in their few telephone conversations. Contact between them had been purposefully limited by the king. E. didn't understand Oba Jaiye's methods, but appreciated his thoroughness. After all, he would have his daughter's welfare in his hands, if she were ever to become queen.

Speaking of Zara, he remembered their last FaceTime. She was in shambles—no makeup, her hair a mess, and her clothes disheveled, but she still maintained an air of elegance about her. She had bedroom eyes, and he couldn't wait to explore what else was under that mess of a woman beyond the glitter and glamour. Obviously, the king understood the heart of a man who was in love. He hadn't realized that he'd crossed over from like to love until he caught a glimpse of the princess behind the pomp and circumstance. Her natural beauty was exquisite and interesting, to say the least. Just as E. was about to take another round down memory lane, something hit his Range Rover SUV and hit it hard enough for it to topple over three times into the forest. The last thing he remembered was his beautiful fiancée's beckoning smile.

The plane was right on time. Her future father-in-law arrived. As soon as he saw Zara, Ezra enveloped her in a big Texas-sized hug. He smelled of Tom Ford's Tobacco Vanille, and she rejoiced in his warmth. He released her, and she was greeted with a huge smile. He walked her back to the SUV, helped her into her seat, and closed the door. He got in on the other side, and the caravan immediately started on its journey back to the compound. The two of them talked about the wellness of family members and the state of the dynasty. Midway on the road back to the compound, all of the security detail's cell phones went off. The caravan pulled over. Princess Zara made an inquiry as to the delay. The team informed her that they were still gathering data and would give her a report in a few minutes. She looked at Ezra, and he offered her a comforting smile and switched the conversation to that of the upcoming nuptials. True to their word, the chaperones were back with a report within minutes.

"Princess Zara," one of the security detail personnel said, "unfortunately the caravan that Mr. Johnson was traveling with was attacked, and he has been kidnapped."

When they arrived back at the palace, there was a different kind of uproar. They had been attacked, and the king had yet to arrive at the palace. Vincent left earlier to meet the king's caravan and discuss kingdom matters. So, the next line of defense was the Alagbatas. They immediately went into action assuming a zero-tolerance protocol. Ezra was beyond himself. However, Zara was the calm that quelled the storm. She assured everyone that when her father arrived, the matter would be handled expeditiously. That seemed to bring peace to E.'s father. She suggested that they pray. After a petition to their heavenly Father, they both felt better about the outcome of the attack. Zara excused herself after dinner and retired to her bedroom early in the evening.

At 1:00 am, with the full moon leading the way, a dark shadowy figure left a hidden exit in the palace compound wall. Inside the palace were several hidden tunnels for this very purpose. Just in case the compound was invaded, the king had insured that there was an alternate way to exit the compound.

Sarki could be one of two places, his father's summer house or the Sambisa Forest. He knew the king would look at his father's place first. He was smarter than that. The Sambisa Forest was his only alternative. As children, they played in that very forest while their fathers hunted for game. But the Sambisa had presently become a dumping ground for murderers and a hiding place for kidnappers.

She was shocked by the sudden change in Sarki's behavior, never in a million years would she have thought that her childhood friend would turn against the kingdom or her for that fact. Perhaps Victoria was right all these years. He was in love with her, or he thought he was. Why else would he kidnap E.? It was all making sense now.

He was not an original thinker. If it worked for someone else, it most likely would work for him, especially when he perfected it for his cause. His strategy was to attack his victims unexpectedly and leverage his advantage through fear and intimidation. Time was of the essence. He was capable of doing anything when he faced the unexpected. E.'s life was in danger and there was no time to waste.

The king arrived at the palace that evening around midnight, and he summoned all of his security forces to the main hall, including the Alagbatas. He was briefed and advised by his head of security to assume an aggressive posture in rescuing the princess's betrothed. He acknowledged the wisdom of that recommendation based on the fact that the only person who had something to gain was Sarki in kidnapping E. It was a retaliation move, not one to acquire wealth. They immediately dispatched a security detail to Sarki's father's house to interrogate his family. The king sent for Ezra to meet him in his study. He offered his genuine condolences over a bottle of their favorite bourbon with a sincere promise that he would bring their son back, alive.

Later that morning, the king decided to survey his kingdom before retiring for a much-needed rest. He needed to know that all was well before he closed his eyes. Everything was on lockdown as expected, but something was missing. The princess wasn't in her bed. He rubbed his eyes to make sure he wasn't hallucinating. He checked again, and she was not there. In a matter of minutes, the entire palace compound was on alert. Princess Zara was gone!

The Sambisa Forest had become a public disgrace to the continent. It was the place where a person could hide a body that would not be found for centuries. The thick foliage and monstrous trees were rumored to be a shelter for the jihadist Boko Haram group and believed to be the hiding place for the kidnapped Chibok schoolgirls. Sarki had chosen well. The forest was huge, and there was no way that she could cover all of it in the short time she had before he did something crazy. When they were children, their parents had several favorite camping spots in the forest—all in the southernmost part. He would need somewhere to hide his captive. So, a campsite would be out of the question, even in these woods. He would need to hide E. in an old abandoned set of buildings or house off of the road somewhere. If that was the case, there would only be one place that he would go, and she was headed in that direction first. Her father had an abandoned training center that he used to train his new security recruits. When the incident happened in 2014 with the Chibok schoolgirls, he closed it down because of the possible bad publicity. No one had been there in over eight years.

Sarki would be aware of its location because of his former position as head of security. She looked at her watch. By foot, she could be there in one hour, but if her memory served her well, there was a motorbike shop up the street where she could borrow a bike. It would cut her travel time in half. She grabbed a motorbike and left an IOU for the owner.

There were five security details searching Dala Dynasty for the princess. The king assumed that the princess was also kidnapped. The Alagbatas barely escaped the king's immediate retribution. Based on the lack of security available at the palace, there was no way they could have been at two places at one time, and Vincent went to bat for them at the risk of losing his own life.

He had never seen the king crazy with worry before. He knew it wasn't because he was afraid for his daughter's life, but it was more about his plan for the kingdom being aborted. They had to find the princess fast, or the king was going to start executing people.

Vincent went on the detail with the king because he was the only one who could handle him. They were headed to northeastern part of Nigeria to the Sambisa Forest. Legend had it that the forest was the gateway to Hell. After a short interrogation, Sarki's younger brother was forced to share his location after the king held a knife to his mother's throat. His father was gagged and tied up in another room after a scuffle with one of the Alagbatas who gave him a slight concussion and a broken arm.

The king arranged for horses to be brought to the forest so that they could better maneuver the unruly flora and dense foliage in the light of dawn. The trip to the forest was an estimated five hours. They made it in two and a half. Enroute, they discussed what would be the best course of action to find Sarki and the hostages. They decided to break up into two groups—one would scout out the northern part of the forest and the other the southern part. Vincent, the king, and Nafisa went to the southern part of the forest.

The owner of the ranch was waiting for them at a motorbike shop not far from the entry to the forest with the horses. It was so dark that the only way they knew the horses were there was by the white glare of their teeth. As she was mounting her horse, Nafisa noticed a piece of paper on the ground. She got off her horse and bent down to pick it up. As she examined the note, she noticed that the handwriting had a feminine flair to it. So, she took it over to Vincent who had his flashlight out, seeking an entry point into the forest. He gasped as he read it. The king immediately demanded to know what was going on.

"Sir, it appears as if the princess was here earlier this evening."

"Say what?"

He passed the note over to the king, and Oba Jaiye literally growled. "The fool girl must have come looking for Sarki on her own. She's no match for him, especially here."

"Sir, I beg the differ," Vincent said. "Remember he trained her in hand-to-hand combat and weapons handling. If anyone knows his strengths and weaknesses, it's the princess."

Nafisa took note of their conversation. It would be important to share this with the other Alagbatas.

"I hope you are right. Since she chose this way to go, she must have an idea where he is. Vincent, do you remember what could possibly be in this area that she may have knowledge of or a facility that would be familiar to both of them?"

Their conversation was interrupted by Nafisa shouting at the men, "The princess went this way."

The king dubiously looked at Vincent and asked, "Can we trust her?"

"Yes."

The small rescue team moved forward quickly under the guidance of the highly effective tracking skills of the Alagbata warrior in search of the princess.

Somewhere around midnight, Ebunoluwa was awakened by the Holy Spirit. Her husband was not shocked to find her at the foot of their bed the next morning on her knees travailing for someone. It was her custom to pray until she felt a release from her heavenly Father when the matter was resolved. He covered her trembling shoulders with a blanket and left the room. She stayed on her knees crying out to God for the princess until midday.

Zara was quite aware of the danger that surrounded her. The forest was known to be a stronghold for the Boko Haram. Its victims were killed, raped, forced into sex slavery, or kidnapped. She must be swift in her rescue and in her retreat. According to the sun's position, she had a maximum of six hours to successfully complete her mission. She abandoned the motor bike a quarter of a mile from the abandoned training camp, and continued on foot. She was dressed like an impoverished young boy from one of the nearby villages. She stopped at a pond and muddied her face and extremities. Even Sarki wouldn't be able to recognize her.

As she drew near to the deserted military compound, she strategically planned her entry and exit. There were several doors that led to the vast main hall, but he wouldn't keep a prisoner there. If her memory served her right, there was an old military bunker in the basement of the building that was used as an escape room for trainees. She was confident that she would find them there. Her exit would have to be the one where there was the least resistance. She didn't know what condition E. would be in. It was her desperate hope that she would still find him alive.

Zara stopped for a moment to pray and ask for God's protection and strength after she realized the magnitude of the task before her.

Simply speaking, she couldn't do this in her own strength and she needed God's divine intervention to accomplish what may have seemed to some as an impossible task. She was soon reminded of a young man with a slingshot and huge faith that killed a giant named Goliath. It was something that amazed her when she read the story in her daily Bible study a couple of days ago. Here was a young man that wasn't even king yet, and God worked through him for the good of his kingdom. If God could do it for him, he could do it for her.

She took a deep breath and proceeded to the basement window that led to the bunker. She broke a small part of the window off, enabling her to remove each individual pane carefully and climbed through it. As she quietly dropped to the floor, she heard two men shouting at each other. The battle of words was so intense that Sarki didn't even notice her approach. E. was the first one to notice her presence, but she motioned for him to be quiet. She looked around for something to hit Sarki with. There was an old military shovel lying next to a massive hole that he was digging. She reached for it with lightning speed and in a matter of seconds hit Sarki on the head with all of her might. He was totally caught off guard and lay unconscious on the floor in a pool of his own blood. She rushed over to release E. from his restraints. His face was a bloody mess, and he had bruises on top of his bruises all over his body, but he was alive. As she cut off the zip ties, he wondered who she was. His right eye was completely closed from swelling.

"Who are you?"

"I am my beloved's, and he is mine," she said hastily removing the ties.

"Zara? Is that you?"

"Yes. We don't have a lot of time. We must leave now!"

"How did you find me?"

She grabbed his arm, placed it around her shoulder, and stuffed her spare gun in his pants pocket. "Here, you just may need this."

"You look like a boy."

"Well, I wasn't trying to win a beauty contest."

"I don't care what you look like, you're one of the most beautiful sights I've ever seen."

"Always the charmer…"

E. was firmly in place on her shoulder. As they approached the door, it swung open almost knocking them down. They were immediately surrounded by the king's rescue squad.

"Stand down. We've got everything under control," the princess commanded.

The rescue team recognized the voice of the princess.

The king spoke, "Obviously not, I go away on kingdom business, and I come home to utter chaos. We will debrief once we are back at the palace compound."

"No one's going anywhere," Sarki said as he pointed a Kalashnikov Machine Gun at the king's head. "That's right, I have enough rounds to kill everyone in here and a grave big enough to bury each of you. And no one will ever be able to find you. Then Dala Dynasty can have the king it deserves."

"You better think very carefully about what you are saying," the king said. "Bigger men have died for less."

"You seem to forget who has the gun."

"What do you want?"

"Your kingdom. And I can't have it until you all are dead."

Sarki pointed the gun at the rescue team and pressed the trigger. They all ran for cover except Nafisa, who moved swiftly and tackled him to the ground, but not before several bullets hit his royal highness in the chest. Zara released E., who fell to the ground with a whimper and ran to her father while Vincent and Nafisa tried to wrestle the machine gun from Sarki. In the heat of the struggle, all three of them found themselves rolling into the freshly dug grave. Vincent managed to escape Sarki's grip, but not before Sarki kicked him in the groin. That left Nafisa to battle a half-crazed Sarki alone.

Suddenly, a shot was fired from a 9 mm Beretta and followed by complete silence. E. stood over the grave which was meant for him with the gun Zara gave him for protection in his hand. Sarki died instantly. Nafisa arm was broken in the struggle, and Vincent helped her out of the grave once he was above ground again. E. stood there mesmerized by the bloody scene before him. Sarki's lifeless eyes stared in shock at a vacant place on the wall of the bunker.

Nafisa looked at E. and said, "It was a justified kill." He hung his head.

"Thanks for saving our lives," Vincent replied. He patted E. on the back and limped over to Zara and the king.

Zara, in a state of terror, tried to comfort her father. She grabbed him in her arms and began to cradle his head in her lap. She looked at her longtime friend and confidante with hope in her eyes. After assessing the king's wounds, Vincent shook his head acknowledging her greatest fears. Her father was dying.

"Father, please don't die."

"Zara, what a silly request," the king mumbled. "When someone shoots you with a machine gun twice, there's a good chance you aren't going to make it out alive."

He looked at E. "Take care of the kingdom. You are in charge now. You are the neck that turns the head of my kingdom."

Zara spoke, "But father..."

"I intended for him to marry you because he is the son I never had," Oba Jaiye continued grasping for breath. "I was desperate..."

"Let's not discuss this now father, we just need to get you to a hospital," Zara sobbed.

"I won't make it... there."

Zara started shaking uncontrollably.

Her father looked at her for the very last time and spoke his final words, "You were the mistake that I could never erase, and God knows that I tried. What a waste of royal seed."

Oba Jaiye took his last breath and died in the arms of his daughter. Vincent reached over and closed his eyes. He picked up the cell phone from the king's waist and called the palace.

After a brief pause, one of the king's security detail answered the phone: "How may I serve you, Your Highness?"

Vincent responded, "Send the king's helicopter to the old Armory in the Sambisa Forest fully armed. Also, send the CSI team and the coroner. The king is dead."

Somewhere in the midst of his conversation the inconsolable wailing of a wounded daughter began and didn't stop until she was in E.'s arms.

CHAPTER 08

The next morning, news trucks from all over the world crowded the palace compound. The press conference was scheduled for noon. The trucks began to arrive at 8:00 a.m. The palace was covered with black ribbons signifying the death of a royal member of the family. Everyone inside the palace walls were given strict instructions not to discuss the details of the king's death with anyone including family members. The palace spin doctors worked to put the finishing details on the press release, so the world would know that Oba Jaiye of Dala Dynasty was dead. Vincent had spent the night securing extra security for the royal family and its staff. He had to prepare the kingdom for the worse in the midst of this great tragedy.

When the rescue team arrived at the palace late that evening, the remaining Alagbata was in full force. They watched a broken princess leave the helicopter wrapped in the arms of her betrothed who carried her like a baby into the palace limping. Vincent and Nafisa followed closely behind. He carried her to the palace elevator. Nafisa pushed the button for the princess's floor, and the doors opened to her suite.

Vincent led E. to her bedroom where he laid her down gently on her bed and assured her he would return. Vincent walked over to his young charge and kissed her on her forehead telling her that all would be well and encouraging her to rest. Zara closed her eyes and was finally able to escape the nightmare after tossing and turning for hours. Somewhere in the night, she was awakened by unfamiliar voices. Agitated by the noise, she opened the door of her bedroom and screamed at the top of her lungs, "Fi awa sil ibikan." Nafisa quickly ushered everyone out of the room. Once the mission was completed, she turned to her queen with great compassion in her eyes and closed the door behind her. Zara went to her disheveled bed and cried herself back to sleep.

Morning came quickly. The queen awoke to the sun shining brightly through her window and the loving voice of her Iya. She spoke softly, "Good morning, my beloved queen." Zara was shocked to see her smiling face. I have been charged with preparing you for your day. She rose from her chair and approached Zara. Let's get you out of yesterday's clothes. She looked down at her tattered t-shirt and khaki pants, which were covered in her father's dried blood. Zara began to wail again. Nafisa rushed into the room, broken arm in a cast, but still prepared to avenge her queen, no matter the physical cost.

Ebunoluwa whispered, "It's okay." She approached Zara's bed and placed her comforting arms around her. "Come my queen. A warm bath will help you feel better. I promise to remain by your side as long as it's necessary. Remember you are not alone, Beloved. Our heavenly Father is here, and He weeps with you. Now, let's get you ready to face this day." Zara allowed Ebunoluwa to lead her to a prepared bath. The queen lowered herself into the water. As her tears mixed with the bubbles, her Iya began to sing comforting hymns that instantly spoke to the hurt and pain that was hidden in her heart. Her father would never love her; he couldn't because he was dead. The queen suddenly grabbed hold of her Iya in desperation squeezing her until her nail prints were etched in her dark skin trying to unravel the puzzle of her pain.

"Iya, why didn't my father love me? I tried to be what he wanted me to be…do what he wanted me to do. I lived my whole life for him. Couldn't he see that?

Her Iya spoke softly, "Beautiful one, unfortunately your earthly father did not recognize the gift God gave him in you. Sometimes because we are so wrapped up in what we think love is, we totally miss its true meaning. Your father was a good ruler, but not a good parent. Unfortunately because of his choices you two will always have an untold love story. But, take my word Beloved, Jehovah Rohi sees all things and he will make sure that what you have lost will be found someday in another way just like he did for Hagar.

The number of news reporters and cameras rivaled the intensity of the news that was to be shared with the world. Low murmurs filled the room as the head of the Council of Elders, appointed to rule in the event of the king's unfortunate demise, hosted the press release. The new queen was there dressed in a Dolce and Gabbana black pant suit, wearing a pair of black Dior shades to shield her grief. Her glamour squad had done a remarkable job, but her burdened posture told the true story. The head of the council read the statement crafted by the public relations team:

During an effort to recover Princess Zara and Ezra Johnson Jr. from their kidnapper, Sarki Acheampong,

Oba Jaiye, King of the Dala Dynasty was killed. His remains will be on display in the palace ballroom for the public to view starting tomorrow, and the burial ceremony will be held two days from now. The coronation of Queen Zara will take place the day after the burial. Additional information will be announced when the plans are finalized. May Queen Zara reign long and prosper!

Queen Zara stepped up to the podium and said, "Dala Dynasty and guests, our hearts are saddened at the passing of our beloved king, but we will continue to be the great nation he made us as a homage to his memory. Thank you."

Zara left the stage followed by her security detail. She heard the head of the counsel say, "That's it for today. We appreciate your respect for the royal family while they are mourning the loss of our beloved king. Check your phones for an updated press release within the hour. Thank you."

The first person to greet her was E. when she returned to her suite, saying, "Are you okay?"

"Yes, she replied. "The kingdom must go on. My father would have wanted it that way."

Ezra Sr. was there also, and he pulled her to him saying, "Thank you for saving my son's life. I am so sorry for the death of your father. As you know, he was the brother I never had. I still can't wrap my head around the series of events that led to his demise. But we will talk about this another time."

Zara replied, "Thank you for coming. If you don't mind, I would like to get some rest."

E. responded, "Certainly. We will talk later."

He hugged her, and their eyes met. She held on a little longer than necessary. He accommodated her. When she pulled away, he reluctantly released her and whispered, "Rest well, Beloved." She nodded and went into her room, got into her night clothes, fell into her bed, and cried herself to sleep.

She was awakened by the persistent ringing of her cellphone. She grappled for it on her nightstand. The number was familiar, but she wasn't sure of the caller's identity. She picked it up and said, "Hello. Who is this?"

"It's Victoria, your long-lost best friend."

"Oh, Vickie, it's great to hear your voice. How are you? I'm so sorry about Sarki."

Victoria responded, "You would say something like that."

"What?

"I would like to come see you, but your Amazon brigade won't let me in. Can you arrange a meeting for us? I'll meet you wherever, whenever, but I need to see you today. Is that possible?"

"Yes. Let me arrange it. Can I reach you at this number?"

"Absolutely. Thank you, Zara. I look forward to seeing you soon," Victoria said before hanging up.

Zara looked at the time on her cellphone and immediately reached out to Nafisa and made arrangements for her and Victoria to meet in her suite dining area. Zara noticed extra security in her suite as the cook set up the dining room table. She questioned Nafisa about it, and her explanation was simple, "You are now the queen of a great nation."

Victoria arrived uncharacteristically early. Two-armed security guards escorted her to Zara's living area. A place that she had been many times before, but the whole atmosphere was now different. Before she was visiting a princess who was her best friend; now she was visiting her queen.

She bowed as is the custom and greeted Zara with, "Ojo dada ni a wa, Your Highness."

Zara responded with a nod followed with, "Get up my dear friend and come give me a hug."

Victoria embraced her, and both women separated with tears streaming down their faces.

"I've missed you, dear friend," Victoria said.

Zara reached for her hand and led her to the dining table saying, "I have missed you too."

They both sat down at a luxurious laid out table with fine linen and china and silver that rivaled that of Buckingham Palace. In addition, there was a table runner with the Dala Dynasty logo boldly embossed on it. Things had changed in her suite while she slept. She queried her dear friend about her urgent request as the first course of a seven-course meal was being served.

Victoria hesitantly began to speak. "I am so very sorry about my cousin's actions. If I had only known his true intentions, I would have warned you earlier. He always led me to believe that he was madly in love with you. I see now, it was a ruse to get close to you so that he could be king one day," Victoria said shaking her head.

"I didn't know the whole story until his brother shared how his father believed a prophetic word from one of the local shamans that his firstborn would be king someday. He has since died, but my uncle filled Sarki's head with that foolishness all of his life. Because our family wasn't in the direct bloodline, they decided that the most feasible way to do that was for Sarki to marry you. When your father made me your permanent playmate and friend, they took it as a confirmation that my cousin was headed for the throne. He studied the kingdom's strengths and weaknesses and designed his career around being a solution to the kingdom's challenges. That's how he became head of security. He convinced the king that Vincent was effective, but his techniques were antiquated in the modern world."

"I see," Zara said. "Well, you know I was interested in him as a potential suitor, but he was always busy with kingdom business. I simply thought he didn't want to be bothered."

"He was interested, but for the wrong reasons."

"But he still wouldn't have been king. His royal designation would have been prince."

The servers brought another course, and the two young women were silent for a period of time as they politely finished it.

"My uncle and Sarki had come up with a plan to keep you barefoot and pregnant so that eventually you would abdicate your throne to him."

Zara stopped her fork midway in the air and said, "He what? What a ridiculous thought. I would never do that."

"I know. I could have told him that," Victoria stated.

They both look at each other and burst out into giggles.

"I've always told you that men are silly. They would rather keep their pride than ask for help. I could have saved him a lot of time and trouble, maybe even his life," Victoria said as she turned her head away from Zara.

The queen reached out and touched her hand saying, "Vickie, unfortunately, we can't change the past. Sarki chose his own destiny, regretfully so. I will miss the good times we had, but I won't ever forget that he is the reason my father is dead. Was this the urgent matter you had to speak to me about?"

"Well not exactly, Zara," Victoria replied. "I came to not only express my condolences but to also let you know that I have always believed that you have what it takes to rule Dala Dynasty. This may have happened a little sooner than you thought, but I can't think of anyone more qualified to take your father's place, and Dala Dynasty will be better for it."

"Thank you so much, my friend," Zara responded.

Victoria placed her napkin on the table saying, "Never forget that I love you, dear friend and nothing can separate us, not even death."

"Are you going somewhere?" Zara asked.

"Our family is relocating to Lagos for obvious reasons," Victoria responded. "Let's schedule that girl's trip we never got to go on sometime soon. How is your oyinbo babe?"

Zara blushed.

"It looks like we will have a lot to talk about on our trip," Victoria said smiling.

"Alright, my dear friend," Zara said, "can I help in any way?"

"No, all the arrangements have been made. The two women arose from the table and met in a parting embrace.

"You will always be my sister," Zara said.

"And you will always be my queen," Victoria emphatically responded. "Wear the crown well, Zara. It was tailor-made for a woman like you. Mo nifẹ rẹ."

"Mo nifẹ rẹ siwaju sii."

Victoria was a wise woman. Her maturity had been a mainstay in their relationship, from the day they first became friends. She had always been there for Zara. No one knew or understood Zara like her dear confidante. It saddened her that they had to part this way, but Victoria was right about one thing: she had rehearsed for this role her entire life. Nevertheless, she would gladly get in a time machine to change the outcome of yesterday's events. Yes, it hurt that her earthly father didn't love her, but her heavenly Father did. She would need to find comfort in that someday.

During the midnight hours after the press conference, Jesus visited her in a vision, placed His loving nail scared hand over her heart, and admonished her the same way he had Joshua—to be strong and courageous. As she had been unquestionably obedient to her earthly father, she would be even more obedient to her heavenly Father. He would help her rule this great kingdom and gain an even greater position in the world than all of her ancestors before her. Zara had lost a lot in a matter of a few days, but she had gained a loving heavenly Father and a kingdom that she would rule for his glory.

The knowledge of her father's closed heart would have destroyed her six months ago, but her Iya had shared with her that God knew what was coming, so He made himself a tangible reality in her life before the enemy could destroy her. Yes, she was aware that there were supernatural forces involved in high places that were working against her and the kingdom. But she would walk in all the power that God was willing to give her to do so. She was not alone, and now she knew that with all of her heart. Que sera sera!

The king was buried beside his ancestors on a dark and dreary day on the Holy Hill. The queen was accompanied by E. and his father, followed by the Alagbatas and Vincent. The people of the Dala Dynasty mourned their leader for three days. The wailing started the morning of the announcement and continued until the hearse left the palace compound for the king's final resting place. His latest wife had to say her goodbyes at the palace compound. He left her his mansion, provided that she relinquished all rights for their children to sit on the throne, and she had to pledge her unconditional allegiance to the queen. All dignitaries and royal emissaries from foreign countries were part of a private viewing the evening before the actual burial. Behind the scenes, the queen was in endless meetings, reassuring their allies that the dynasty would continue to foster the diplomatic relations that the king had formed during his reign. The headlines chronicled the tragic loss and the events surrounding a nation losing a king.

Security was at an all-time high because of the massive number of paparazzi covering the funeral. The common people were relegated to the foot of the hill, while the dignitaries and the governing council were allowed to follow the family to the gravesite. Each member of the funeral march carried a purple violet in remembrance of the king's love for them.

The king's mahogany coffin was carried to the gravesite by his security staff. The royal banner draped the final resting place of its beloved champion. For the king who adored his country, they adored him back today. When Cardinal Arinze began the final committal prayer, there wasn't a dry eye on the hill.

> *"Eternal rest grant unto our beloved king, O Lord, and let perpetual light shine upon him. May his soul and the souls of all the faithful departed, through the mercy of God, rest in peace. We, therefore, commit this body to the ground, earth to earth, ashes to ashes, dust to dust, in sure and certain hope of the Resurrection to eternal life. Amen."*

Observers saw the tangible grief of their queen, but little did they know that the grief they observed was peppered with regret. Her father was gone, and all hope of having his love was now being buried with him. Zara fell to her knees, ripping off her clothes and clawing at the dirt as the pain of her father's rejection captured her heart. E. fell beside her and whispered comforting words into her ear, but it wasn't enough. He looked up helplessly at his father, whose tears clouded his vision. The Alagbatas formed a tighter circle around the royal delegation, protecting their queen from the public eye. Her wailing resumed this time with a piercing scream that could be heard down the hill. When every heart on that hill could break no more, Ezra Sr. bent down to embrace Zara, and the following words came out of his mouth: "I love you, and you are worthy of that love. I give it to you freely." God used Ezra's words to pierce the pain that was engulfing her. Zara's spirit rose and grabbed the warmth of his words, and the healing began. The wailing stopped, and she found the inner strength that the Holy Spirit appropriated to rise to her feet and straighten her skirt and suit jacket. Immediately, there were handkerchiefs and hugs from those who loved her. Even more amazing was the appearance of Iya beside Vincent, her solemn bronze face filled with compassion. She bowed to the ground in humble submission, saying, "Your majesty, today God has made you a queen. We, your people, need you desperately. May He give you the strength to walk in your anointing. Remember, "Weeping may endure for a night, but joy will come in the morning." Ebunoluwa rose to her feet, turned, and disappeared into the crowd.

The dark bows had been removed from the Palace Compound gates and replaced with the purple and gold ceremonial banners of the Dala Dynasty. This was the day that the queen officially acceded to the throne, and the Dala Council of Elders would conduct the Coronation ceremony with the blessing of Cardinal Arinze. Zara's heart was tender from her father's burial the day before. Even though it was customary for a country to wait several months after the death of its leader to have a coronation, she had to assume the role of queen quickly because her nation was in its most vulnerable state without an apparent designated leader.

Things were happening too fast. Her whole life had been a dress rehearsal for this moment. She never thought it would be so soon after she graduated from college. Zara had envisioned herself traveling the world and flirting with interesting strangers until it was necessary to get married. Her father always had things under control; if they ever got out of control, his constituents knew they wouldn't stay that way for long. And then there was the matter of her upcoming nuptials. They were scheduled to get married in six months. They hadn't had much of a courtship, and she didn't know if that would change with her new responsibilities. Sarki had made such a mess of things. Now he and her father were dead. The queen squeezed her eyes shut as hard as she could, trying to wipe out the mental picture of her father and Sarki's last moments.

Zara made a mental note not to stay focused on the things she couldn't change. The best position for her was to move forward. Her coronation gown and the matching gemstones lay on her bed. Nafisa was sticking closer than normal, so there was no ducking out of the suite onto the palace grounds. She could use fresh air, but propriety would not allow it. She sighed. Her glam team would be there within the hour anyway. She went to her favorite chair, put her head back on the back, and closed her eyes again, but this time she was praying.

A formal midday event was not the custom of the dynasty, but the circumstances dictated that the coronation occur as soon as possible. At the elevator that leads to the ballroom, E. and Ezra Sr. meet the queen. Her beloved kissed her forehead and raved about her being the most beautiful creature in the Dala Dynasty. His bold and bodacious praise did not go unnoticed by the event's onlookers, and Zara blushed profusely. She extended her arm to him to escort her into the ballroom. His father took her other arm. The council and a representative from each tribe in the dynasty followed them. The event wasn't as glamorous as the betrothal gala, but it was as festive as the series of events preceding it would allow. The only cameras permitted were those of the palace media. The queen entered the room, and everyone stood to honor her.

A classical rendition of the Dala Dynasty Anthem was playing. She was dressed in a velvet purple coat that covered her princess-cut pearl white gown underneath. Her braids were put in a crown twist updo and intertwined with strands of gold that matched her dangling pearl and gold earrings. Her makeup rivaled any model on a Paris runway, and she wore matching satin pumps that complimented her dress. Once she arrived at the dais, Nafisa took her cloak, and E. escorted her to the center of the room, where she kneeled, and the ceremony began.

The council elders administered the proclamation recognizing Zara as the new queen of the Dala Dynasty. Cardinal Arinze held the Bible as the new queen said the oath that sealed the deal on her royal assignment. The Cardinal then prayed and anointed the queen for service. The council leader, the honorable Mobolaji Nwadike, presented the queen with a royal sash and crowned her with a bejeweled crown with rubies, emeralds, diamonds, and sapphires in the diadem. The queen was then led to a throne that rivaled her father's size but was more feminine in appearance with its satin-covered purple pillows and gold cushioned back padding. As she officially took the seat of power, the room exploded with applause. The ceremony concluded with a brief speech from the queen about her plans for the dynasty, followed by a closing procession filled with the pomp and circumstance befitting the occasion. There was a brief reception in the small ballroom, where Queen Zara received the congratulations and well wishes of the dignitaries, both domestic and foreign. By mid-evening, the queen was exhausted. She excused herself, but the celebration continued until the following day. E. walked her back to her suite and bid her sweet dreams and a good night. She hugged and thanked him for his support, then disappeared into her suite. Her handmaiden assisted her in shedding the royal attire of the day. There was a knock on the door, and Vincent asked for the crown to secure it in the royal safe. Her handmaiden brought her the imitation, which was an exact duplicate. The queen marveled at the genius of her father. Even now, his protocols were working for the betterment of the kingdom. Earlier, the palace media department had run a documentary about Oba Jaiye of Dala on the dynasty television station, which included a farewell message that supported her reign as Dala Dynasty's new ruler. At least she could rest tonight, knowing that her crown was secure because of his foresight, even if her heart wasn't.

It was three days before E. could get on the queen's schedule. He was frustrated. When he finally got to talk with her, they were constantly interrupted. He had had enough and ordered everyone out of the room before confronting the queen about her limited availability. She was caught off guard by his response and assumed a confrontational posture to combat his anger. When he finally ran out of steam, she was ready with what she felt was a proper response.

"My father arranged our marriage based on what he felt was best for the kingdom at that time. Unfortunately, he is no longer with us. I am prepared to release you from your betrothal contract with a reasonable dowry. I am sorry, but my father has left me with the huge responsibility of running a kingdom. It is obvious that I no longer have time for courtship. I say this with the utmost regret, but I presently have no room in my life for coddling a grown man. You are dismissed. Nafisa will escort Mr. Johnson to his room, see him safely to the royal airport, and put him on the plane back to his homeland, America. Clear the room NOW!"

"Yes, your highness."

"Tell my assistant I will be ready for my next appointment in ten minutes. Thank you."

E. stood there flabbergasted, wondering what type of hell he had just entered.

Nafisa whispered, "Sorry," and led E. out of the queen's office to his room. He asked her if he could call his father. She nodded her approval. He was in a total state of shock. His father rushed into his room while packing and asked E. what was happening.

"The queen has banished me from the dynasty and is sending me back to America."

"What?"

"Yes. She said that she has the power as queen to nullify our contract, and now that she's in charge, she doesn't have time for courtship."

"That doesn't sound like Zara. She must have been provoked. What did you do?"

"I told her I wasn't happy with having to make an appointment to see her, and she lost her cool."

"There must be more."

E. was silent.

Ezra Sr. looked at Nafisa and asked her what had happened.

She hesitated to respond, but it didn't appear that anyone would do anything unless she did, so she let it rip. "He busted into the queen's office, full of tribal dignitaries, and commanded everyone to leave. Then he yelled at her at the top of his lungs for fifteen minutes."

His father shook his head, saying, "I guess I'll see you in Texas next week. It looks like I'll be doing some relationship repair in the meantime." He turned on his heels and stomped out of the room, mumbling, "Darn kids."

E. looked at Nafisa and said, "Thanks."

"My obligation is to my queen. You would have been eating carpet if we didn't have history."

"Why are African women so eager to emasculate a man?"

"A real man can hold on to his masculinity wherever he goes."

"So you are an expert on men now?"

"I have seven brothers, which qualifies me for expert status. She looks at her Apple Watch; the plane will leave in 90 minutes. The queen has yet to execute someone, but you are a prime candidate." She chuckles.

"She wouldn't."

"If I were you, I wouldn't want to find out."

He throws his clothes in a suitcase, slams it shut, and says, "Let's go!"

Americans always have to have the last word. She shakes her head.

E. still couldn't believe he was headed back home. In about an hour, his plane would touch down in Houston. What was he to do now? Twelve hours later, he had rehearsed what happened in Zara's office a million times. He's never seen her like this before. His almost-fiancé was a tiger when she wanted to be. She reminded him of someone—her father. OMG!

Zara spent the rest of the day repairing the damage that E. had done to her reputation during his brief temper tantrum. She instructed the Palace Media Department to release a statement about the dissolution of the betrothal contract between them, but not before half of the kingdom knew of the lover's quarrel in the queen's office and the fact that E. had been escorted to the royal airport and sent home in less than 24 hours. This move quelled the rebellion that was starting to brew among the pobu of the dynasty. Some people thought the queen lacked the maturity to run the kingdom. This brought a brief reprieve to the quiet storm. There was peace in the land as the young queen spread her royal wings and attempted to fly with a broken heart.

CHAPTER 09

Ropo Achempong was a proud man. Life hadn't been kind to him lately; his son had been labeled a traitor and murdered. As a result, his entire family had to relocate to Lagos, and his beloved wife had not spoken a word since news of their son's death had reached their ears. He would not acknowledge the pain that propelled him to overthrow the queen of the Dala Dynasty's throne, but he could acknowledge his hatred for her and all she was. After all, if she had only been complicit in his plan, none of this would have happened. His son was the jewel of the Dala Dynasty, and she crushed him into a million pieces. Now she would pay with her life.

Her imbecilic father had terrorized his family to find out where Sarki was. He watched the king threaten to kill his wife if his youngest son wouldn't tell him the location of his brother. Ropo was comforted when he heard that the king was killed by his son. It was a just reward: a life for a life. He deserved no less, especially after he replaced his son on the throne with an Oyinbo. Dala should have been ruled by someone from the continent, not some foreigner who knew nothing of their country and had disdain for its people. He recently showed his true intentions by disrespecting the queen's office and guests.

It wasn't hard for him to start the rumor that she was incompetent. Her age and gender contributed to the falsehood that originated on his ranch. Just the thought of leaving everything he'd spent a lifetime building would have been enough to want to annihilate her. Still, she compounded that desire with the false accusation of attempted rape. Yes, she would pay dearly for her lies. Taking the kingdom from Queen Zara would be easier than taking candy from a baby, and he would give his very life if he had to see that day become a reality.

It took Ezra several days to get an audience with the queen. She was extremely apologetic, but it was apparent that she was operating on fumes. The plastic smile and hooded eyes indicated that she wasn't resting well. Zara needed a spiritual armor-bearer. She was carrying the kingdom's weight without prioritizing her self-care. Every leader had to find a balance, or they would eventually break. Based on his experience, she was headed for a hospital bed in about six months. He had to do something,

That fool son of his could have helped her. After all that training, he still didn't understand his role as her prince. He was to protect, serve, and love her as a helper in her role as a queen. Their home and his career were where he should reign. He's heard that the king's wife showed up one morning at the palace compound, refusing to live in the mansion after the funeral because she said the king was visiting her in her dreams. The queen had her and her family move from the mansion to a house of her choosing in Lagos with a hefty check that covered the purchase of the king's old residence. Ezra had been moved out of his suite into the king's old room. Queen Zara was remodeling the entire west wing. It was to become her new residence. She was too accessible at the Palace Compound. Ezra agreed with her decision; she needed a place where she could just be Zara. And, now, he was sitting in front of her, and the Holy Spirit was tugging on his heart to become more than her father's blood brother but a father to the fatherless. She asked him a question.

"Have you heard from E.?"

"No. But I have talked to Julia. He seems to be doing as well as you are."

Her chin quivered. "What do you mean?"

"You love my son?"

She hesitated for a second and then whispered, "Yes."

"I thought so. Well, he loves you too, and I suspect he has difficulty digesting what happened between you two. And I am assuming you are also troubled as a result of your quarrel... Am I correct?"

"Yes."

"So, what are you two going to do about this mess?"

The queen sat back in her chair, looked up at the ceiling, and responded, "I don't know."

"Somebody's going to have to say they are sorry eventually, or you two will go on to live your entire lives regretting that you didn't finish what you started."

"It sounds like you are talking from experience."

"I am."

"What would you have me do?"

"Nothing you don't want to do."

"I am caught between a great precipice surrounded by a vast ocean. All my life, I have been a tool that was fashioned for one man's purpose. Now that he is gone, I can see clearly that his decisions, although wise, were not necessarily made with the right motives. Marrying E. was one of those things. My heart would have me jump off the cliff into the nearest boat and sail to America to fall into the arms of my beloved. But the part of me that wonders if I am loveable just because I am Zara speaks much louder than my heart."

She sits up in the chair and looks at Ezra eyeball to eyeball, saying, "I will not give my heart to another man who is more interested in what I can do for him than in who I am as a woman, a wife, and a potential mother of his children. I will not be ruled by the whims and dictates of a man's flesh. If I can't have all of him, heart included, I don't want him."

Ezra briefly contemplated her answer and then said, "Let's pray."

Later that evening, Ezra called Julia to check on his son.
"He's been in his room all week, barely eating, but I am happy to say he hasn't left the house."

"I see. What do you think about this thing between him and Zara?"

"I think they both need to grow up. This won't be the last time they have a disagreement. If they were married, they would be nowhere to run to. They'd have to stay together until they figured it out."

"Do you think it's redeemable?"

"I sure hope so. In the thirty years that he's been around, I've never seen him act like this about a girl. If someone rejected him, he'd either fight until he won her over or move on to the next one. I believe he didn't get a chance to fight for Zara because she returned him to America faster than he could say, "I'm sorry." Why are you asking me all of these questions?"

I think there's still a chance for a reconciliation between these two. At least, that's what I'm praying for.

"Didn't she cancel the betrothal contract?"

"Yes."

"So how is something like that restored?"

"Unfortunately, it can't be, but that doesn't stop one from seeking the other's hand in marriage. Their still both very single."

"I see. So do you think she would come to America?"

"No. She's too busy, and I think she wants to be chosen instead of being told that she must marry someone."

"Really? Well, you know our son can be very charming."

"I think it's going to take that and a lot more."

"What do you mean?"

"He's got to prove to her that he loves Zara for Zara, not just because she is a queen or wealthy or because her father wanted him to do it."

"So, Queen Zara wants a Prince Charming on a white horse experience?"

"I suppose so. One thing is certain: Her few weeks in office have matured her beyond her 21 years. She needs a real man not threatened by her position or power to stand beside her as an equal partner in marriage. You know our son better than anyone; do you think he could do it?"

"Sure, once he gets beyond his pride."

"How long do you think that will take?"

"Well, I'm sure it will be any day now. I think I heard him whimpering a day or two ago. I hate to see him like this, but I know God is in the midst of this."

"I've been praying for the both of them."

"Me too."

"So, when are you coming back now that you've talked with her?"

"I should be back this weekend."

"When can we expect you to come to visit E.?"

"Probably Sunday. I'll need a lot of divine assistance when I do."

Julia giggled. "See you on Sunday then. Are you coming for dinner?"

"Sure. Tell that big bear of a husband of yours that I'm bringing some of the king's best bourbon."

"Church and Bourbon, some things never change."

Ropo's efforts were accelerated when the king's foolish wife was convinced that her eldest daughter had as much right to the throne as Queen Zara. Even though she was a minor, Ropo told her that he would support her as a temporary replacement in her stead until her daughter came of age. That got her attention. She saw visions of making the Dala Dynasty the world's fashion capital. Instead of the world's top designers going to Paris to showcase their masterful designs, they would come to the Palace Compound, all under her skillful leadership. She said, "Yes."

They started a vicious marketing campaign against the queen in some of the major Nigerian gossip rags that were known for scandalous tidbits on the lives of celebrities and influencers. She was labeled "The Virgin Queen." They hired major Nigerian influencers to stir up the pot about her lack of sexual prowess; they even started a rumor that she had a secret life as a lesbian. The citizens of the Dala Dynasty did not know how to handle the negative publicity, and they barely knew their queen. Hence, a large majority of the population believed the hype. They didn't have anything to combat the lies. The other half, her staunch supporters, did everything in their power to ignore the lies, but eventually, the rumors got bigger and bigger.

This was the fuel that ignited the bravado of a small militia of disgruntled citizens, who, to Pobo's delight, decided to attack the compound. Their plot was discovered before they could carry it out and stopped, but the match had been lit. Their actions emboldened others to stand against the queen and the palace.

This protest extended to the Palace Compound walls. Any new policies that she would try to implement were met with opposition. Even members of the Elders Council took the public's side and questioned the queen on every move she made. Vincent increased security, and the Palace Media Team was vigilant in their responses to these attacks, but the people's hearts had been soured by the national attention this was bringing to their kingdom, and they wanted someone to pay for their fallen status in the world's eyes.

Queen Zara had never experienced such an attack before in her life. She would often meet with her inner circle for advice, but there had been peace in Dala Dynasty for a hundred years, and they were as clueless as she was. She'd only been in office for less than four months, and all hell was breaking loose.

The straw that broke the camel's back was when she received a telephone call from the American Embassy requesting a private audience with her as soon as possible. The American ambassador brought news of a growing militia and aerial pictures of a large group of soldiers camped on Shike Hill who was well armed. He informed the queen that her life was in imminent danger. He recommended that she prepare the country's military forces for a civil war. This militia would have 1,000 men before the summer if things continued. They were also recruiting mercenaries to lead this swelling human war machine. When asked if he knew the mastermind behind this tyrannical breach of loyalty, he provided her with a picture, saying, "This man." The ambassador was pointing to a picture of Ropo Achempong. He glared at the camera as if he knew she would see it someday. He reminded the queen that America would stand by their treaty and could assist if needed. He rose from his seat, wished her well, and left the room.

War was inevitable. The queen knew that beyond a shadow of a doubt. Her father had never had to go to war, so this wasn't something that he'd included in his instructional repertoire. He's naive to think she wouldn't have to face this possibility. She was at a loss, and her heart ached for her people and the comforting arms of her beloved E. The pain that gripped her heart caused her to fall to her knees, and she sought her heavenly father's advice, as she'd been taught to do by her Iya.

Later, preparing for bed, she was led to open her Bible to Psalm 35. Here's what she read:

> *1 Contend, Lord, with those who contend with me;*
> *fight against those who fight against me.*
> *2 Take up shield and armor;*
> *arise and come to my aid.*
> *3 Brandish spear and javelin*
> *against those who pursue me.*
> *Say to me,*
> *"I am your salvation."*
> *4 May those who seek my life*
> *be disgraced and put to shame;*
> *may those who plot my ruin*
> *be turned back in dismay.*
> *5 May they be like chaff before the wind,*
> *with the angel of the Lord driving them away;*

6 may their path be dark and slippery,
with the angel of the Lord pursuing them.
7 Since they hid their net for me without cause
and without cause dug a pit for me,
8 may ruin overtake them by surprise—
may the net they hid entangle them,
may they fall into the pit, to their ruin.
9 Then my soul will rejoice in the Lord
and delight in his salvation.
10 My whole being will exclaim,
"Who is like you, Lord?
You rescue the poor from those too strong for them,
the poor and needy from those who rob them."
11 Ruthless witnesses come forward;
they question me on things I know nothing about.
12 They repay me evil for good
and leave me like one bereaved.
13 Yet when they were ill, I put on sackcloth
and humbled myself with fasting.
When my prayers returned to me unanswered,
14 I went about mourning
as though for my friend or brother.
I bowed my head in grief
as though weeping for my mother.
15 But when I stumbled, they gathered in glee;
assailants gathered against me without my knowledge.
They slandered me without ceasing.
16 Like the ungodly they maliciously mocked;
they gnashed their teeth at me.
17 How long, Lord, will you look on?
Rescue me from their ravages,

my precious life from these lions.
18 I will give you thanks in the great assembly;
among the throngs I will praise you.
19 Do not let those gloat over me
who are my enemies without cause;
do not let those who hate me without reason
maliciously wink the eye.
20 They do not speak peaceably,
but devise false accusations
against those who live quietly in the land.
21 They sneer at me and say, "Aha! Aha!
With our own eyes we have seen it."
22 Lord, you have seen this; do not be silent.
Do not be far from me, Lord.
23 Awake, and rise to my defense!
Contend for me, my God and Lord.
24 Vindicate me in your righteousness, Lord my God;
do not let them gloat over me.
25 Do not let them think, "Aha, just what we wanted!"
or say, "We have swallowed him up."
26 May all who gloat over my distress
be put to shame and confusion;
may all who exalt themselves over me
be clothed with shame and disgrace.
27 May those who delight in my vindication
shout for joy and gladness;
may they always say, "The Lord be exalted,
who delights in the well-being of his servant."
28 My tongue will proclaim your righteousness,
your praises all day long.

Queen Zara slept like a baby that night with the assurance that her heavenly father was with her and that he never lost a battle.

Queen Zara met with her security team and military leadership the following day to discuss her defense strategy. It was obvious that a civil war was unavoidable. They had an advantage because their security acumen was one of the best in the world. But their military forces could not preempt an attack from their adversaries. This made them sitting ducks. Her strategy was to assume a proactive position. The rebels were building an army that hadn't quite reached its maximum capacity. Now was the time to strike.

The men were literally in a state of shock. Their queen had barely seen her 22nd birthday, and she was advocating an aggressive defense posture. Vincent was the first to speak.

"Queen Zara, if I'm hearing you correctly, you would like us to prepare the military forces to attack the rebels?"

"Yes. I need an updated status on our troops within the hour. We will meet again at 3:00 pm to solidify our next course. We will aggressively attack any threat to this regime. I pledged to do so, and as the commander of ALL of our armed forces, I am declaring war. Any questions?"

Everyone nodded their affirmation.

She left the room, followed by each of the Alagbatas warriors in a stately procession. They held their heads high with pride.

CHAPTER 10

E. was lying on his bed, contemplating his next move. His father visited him a couple of weeks ago and brought with him a check from the Dala Dynasty for his inconvenience. He tore the check-up and threw it in the trash. His father simply shook his head and walked out of the room.

Julia's husband, Curtis, was weary of E.'s nomadic behavior and designed an intervention. He turned his eldest teenage son loose on his older brother. It started with him constantly intruding on his brother's privacy while collecting needed items from his room. Their next action was to grease up his dumbbells while he was asleep. Exercise had become a place of refuge for E. during his recovery from Zara's perceived rejection. Half of Curtis' weight equipment was in E.'s temporary bedroom. The next morning, when he went to start his daily exercise routine, he was greeted with a surprise, and Curtis and his eldest were greeted with several choice explicitness.

He threw the dumbbells out into the hallway with a grunt. He went into the bathroom and wiped his hands off on his brother's bath towel, then headed back into the room to start a new routine.

Later that day, when his supper was delivered, he grunted a muffled *"thank you"* to his mother and put the plate of food on the dresser. He pulled up a chair to start his dinner. Firmly positioned, he took his first bite and was greeted by an extremely hot sensation that flooded his mouth. He screamed at the top of his lungs, ran to the bathroom shower, turned on the cold-water full force, got in, and opened his mouth. His mother ran up the steps and found him in the shower, soaked. She asked him, "What's the matter?"

His look accused her before the words came out. "You put hot sauce in my food. You know I don't like it," he said as involuntary tears ran down his cheeks.

She simply said, "No, I didn't. It's about time you took a shower." She turned around and went back to her kitchen. As he entered his bedroom, he could hear snickering behind his brother's door.

That was it. He was leaving TODAY! He didn't know where he was going, but he was going somewhere other than this hellhole. E., dripping wet, threw his clothes into his suitcase, slammed it shut, and headed for the door. The telephone rang as he reached the bottom step. His mother answered and said,

"Hello. Oh, Hi, Ezra."

"Yes, he's here. It's for you..." She handed the telephone to E., glaring at him because he was dripping water all over her newly scrubbed foyer.

"Hi, Dad, what's up?"

"Dala Dynasty is going to war. Vincent is sending Queen Zara's jet to pick me up. It arrives in an hour. If you love Zara, you will be on that plane with me. Son, she needs us. Please don't make the mistake I made with your mother and lose the only woman you've ever loved, perhaps forever."

"Pops…" The telephone went dead.

Queen Zara sent an expedition of twelve spies to Shike Hill. They returned several days later, affirming the report of the American ambassador. This solidified her plan to conduct a preemptive attack on the rebels. To the angst of Vincent and several of her council leaders, she was leading the strike. The palace media team propagated a story about her visiting various cities in the dynasty on a goodwill tour. One of those cities was at the base of Shike Hill, Kano.

They were scheduled to leave the Dala Dynasty Palace Compound in the morning. It would take approximately eight hours by car to get to Kano, where the queen was scheduled to give a state of the dynasty address that evening. In her armored Mercedes-Benz S-Guard 600, Vincent, Nafisa, and the head of the Council of Elders sat. The address was to be televised all over the dynasty. Someone deliberately leaked to the paparazzi that the queen's next stop was the bush, where she would spend several days visiting local tribal chiefs. News reporters jammed the conference center where the queen would give her address. She was dressed in a rose-print Shantung blazer over a black turtleneck, and black slacks with a matching turban sprinkled with complementing jewels. She accented this ensemble with black Christian Louboutin pumps with red soles. As she approached the podium, the room erupted in applause. The media team also ensured that the room was filled with supporters by extending private invitations. Zara spoke for 25 minutes, starting with the continued economic growth of the dynasty and ending with a joke about her private life. "Ladies and gentlemen, as you know, a queen's job is a 24/7 endeavor. I wish I had time to do a fraction of what they say about me in the tabloids. Oh, what a dreary life I lead." She smiled and said, "Thank you for coming. Long live Dala Dynasty!"

The corresponding response from the audience was, "Long live the Queen!"

Later that evening, as she was resting, she flipped on the television to access the results of her speech on the late-night news. Nafisa suddenly appeared in her suite, took the remote from the queen, and petitioned her to seek a good night's sleep instead of causing controversy. She reluctantly agreed, laid her head on the pillow, and drifted off. She was awakened too early the next morning for their journey. She showered, and when she returned, her fatigues were laid out on the bed, and a shiny new pair of boots were on the floor. Zara mused over the fact that she had never been in a military conflict before. This cloak-and-dagger scrimmage had the potential to test her true capacity as a warrior. She wondered how she would fare. She hadn't lived enough of a life to know its joys. Her calling prevented her from experiencing some of the niceties of life that other women enjoyed. She stopped mid-thought because she was being summoned to join her military entourage. Yet she knew that this was a conversation she would need to conclude with herself later. She sighed. "Leadership is lonely; it's a requirement of the business I'm in." It wasn't a pleasant surprise for her.

They arrived at the ranch that was their military headquarters 24 hours later. The small band of troops was being prepared for the quiet invasion of Ropo's military operation with additional education about the geographical area, what had been gathered about the rebels, and military mountain training. The assault was scheduled to be implemented in 48 hours. The men appeared to be ready. In her quiet time, Queen Zara would study Judges 4, where the Prophetess/Judge Deborah led the Israelite troop to victory. She memorized Psalm 35 and prayed for each of the members of the small militia by name. She spent numerous hours in her tent on her knees, seeking God's guidance, and he did not disappoint her. On the day of the assault, she had an infectious, unusual peace. She had concluded that even if it cost her her life, her country would still be free!

A dark figure ran towards the plane's door as it was about to leave the airport. The co-pilot came to ask the chancellor if he wanted to investigate, and he acknowledged his consent. The co-pilot came back with his son's Texas driver's license. He told him to open the door because his son would join them for the trip to the Dala Dynasty. His father's heart sighed with relief. The boy wasn't as pigheaded as he thought he was, and to God be the glory for that!

The small military caravan was moving aggressively through the night towards their mountainous destination when they went through a rural city. Queen Zara was enjoying the starlit display from her window when she noticed something peculiar. One of the huts had a window open, catching the night air, and the queen glimpsed a young mother nursing her baby. Memories of a lost love came flooding back into her breaking heart, and a single tear ran down her cheek. It was the only vulnerability she would allow herself during this call to battle. She mourned the possibility—the probability—that she would never hold a child to her breast like that woman. Her soul ached with regret, not because of her calling but because of its cost.

An angel of the Lord caught that tear and took it directly to the Lord of Lords, and he instantly interceded for the queen, saying,

> *"For I know the plans I have for you," declares the Lord, "plans to prosper you and not to harm you, plans to give you hope and a future" (Jeremiah 29:11).*

The small military caravan had reached the point where traveling in an automobile would be extremely dangerous. Queen Zara suspected this was why Ropo picked Shike Hill as his base of operations. They had horses delivered to their campsite to better climb the rocky terrain. It took them three days to complete their arduous journey to their final campsite.

The Alagbatas were her constant companions. They never let her get out of their sight. The night before the advance on Ropo's camp, the queen gathered her troops around her and shared the importance of their success. She also thanked them for loving the dynasty so much that they would fight for it and their families. She assured them that their efforts would be rewarded. She also placed a $1 million bounty on Ropo's head, dead or alive. She asked the military chaplain to say a prayer. They all retired to their tents afterward.

Vincent came to visit her before he retired. They reviewed their battle strategy and discussed alternate plans if things did not go as planned. He told her that Ezra had arrived at the compound to assume his role as chancellor for as long as he was needed there. She sighed with relief. His response was a smile. She asked him what was so funny. He simply said, "Have a good night, my princess."

He then left her tent, shaking his head in wonder at the woman she had become. Her military commanders were astonished at her foresight. She comprehended their recommendations for the offensive attack and helped them too often choose the most humane choices. She had prepared the palace hospital before they left to handle casualties from allies and enemies. She also had the prison cleaned, painted, and refurbished for prisoners. The queen also alerted the air force to be on call to transport all severely injured soldiers to the nearest medical facility.

Her commanders openly praised her for her intelligence and leadership skills. They secretly wondered how she would perform in an actual battlefield scenario. Vincent and Nafisa shared knowing glances during these conversations. They knew their queen and had no questions about her commitment to her beloved Dala Dynasty. She would die for her country if need be.

The morning came too soon. The queen was up before dawn, preparing her backpack for the trip. She'd spent more time on the firing range over the last few days. The Alagbatas had started their training exercises in a separate part of the campsite. They aimed to help prepare the queen for battle. To everyone's surprise, except Nafisa, the queen was quite capable of holding her own, especially in hand-to-hand combat. She remembered Sarki's favorite mantra during her training: *"Travel light, travel right."* She immediately cast his image from her mind and moved on quickly to preoccupy herself with her preparation. Now was not the time to hash out her feelings about their lost friendship. He was dead, and unfortunately, his father wanted the dynasty to pay for his death, even if he was in the wrong. Because of it, she was now on a battlefield, preparing to restore the dignity of her country. She closed her eyes and whispered a quick prayer for the relief of her troubled soul. Once she felt God's peace again, she got up from her sleeping bag and left her tent to lead the attack.

Vincent had given the Alagbatas strict instructions to guard the queen with their lives. He reminded them of their sworn oath to protect her. They all acknowledged his command and assumed their positions at the front of the armed forces. The queen refused to ride in the back of the troops, even after the commander insisted that she do so. He looked at Vincent and shrugged his shoulders, saying, "She's the queen."

The queen rode her Russian Arabian up to the front, with the Alagbatas flanking her left and right. The commander just shook his head and rode back to his troops, mumbling, "Stubborn," just like her father.

They were about to embark on their journey when shouts from the back of the battalion alerted the Alagbatas that a rider was coming to the front.

Nafisa shouted, "Akiyesi!" The women all drew their spears to prepare for battle, like synchronized swimmers preparing to start a meet. It was a sight to be seen. The men who doubted their ability to excel in battle had a sudden change of heart. Vincent broke formation and greeted the rider before allowing him an audience with the queen. He signaled his approval, shouting, "Let the rider by. He has an important message for the queen." Zara was busy looking at her watch, wondering how much time they had before it would be too late to attack Ropo's camp. She looked up to greet the rider, and her heart stopped.

A long-haired muscular version of E. rode up on her father's Black Stallion; blue eyes focused on the object of his desire.

Nafisa shouted, "Ni irorun!" The Alagbatas 'spears were placed back in their sheaths. E. asked Nafisa if he could ride next to the queen.

She looked directly at Zara, and she nodded her approval. He maneuvered his horse with expert skill to land directly beside the queen.

She looked at him, giving him the consummate professional response. "I understand you have a message for me of great importance."

He obstinately replied with heartfelt conviction. "I refuse to let the woman I love go into battle without being by her side. "Do not press me to leave you or to turn back from following you! Where you go, I will go; Where you lodge, I will lodge; your people shall be my people, and your God my God. Where you die, I will die… there will I be buried" (Ruth 1:16 - 17).

EPILOGUE

Queen Zara led her troops into a victorious battle that day. The history books would later call it the Battle of Shike Hill. The unfortunate consequence was that Ropo escaped, which did little to damper the queen's enthusiasm. On the last day of the battle, E. got on his knees and asked the queen to marry him. The entire camp cheered when she said, "Yes."

ABOUT THE AUTHOR

Sharon C. Jenkins

Sharon C. Jenkins is the Inspirational Principal for The Master Communicator's Writing Services. She started her journey as a poet, graduated to a playwright, and is now an award-winning, bestselling author, blogger, and podcaster. Her solo projects consists of the following titles: Beyond the Closet Door, Christ's Rescue from Abuse, Authorpreneur-ship: The Business Start-Up Manual for Authors, and The Super Author Journal, The Super Authordom Notebook, and a host of e-books tailored for authors on such topics as writing, marketing, time management, and publishing.

Her most recent print releases for authors are compilations titled, Are you a Super Author? and You Can Be a Super Author Too! These books have "How to Get It Done" stories of seasoned authorpreneurs loaded with the hiccups and tips from their journey. They were intentionally designed to be a literary inspiration for authors interested in starting a business in writing.

Sharon has been a featured blogger on Huffington Post, The Good Men Project, Self-Published Author, Afrovibesradio.com, and Book Marketing Tools. She also hosts her podcast Luminance (available on most podcast platforms) where she sheds the light on people who are doing good in the world. Sharon is also a board member of the award-winning Brilliant Women in Film, whose creative team directed and produced her mini- documentary, The Birthing of a Book Baby. She has been the conference host for multiple writers' conferences around the nation. She has also been a featured panelist or speaker at national, regional, and local events such as the national NAACP and Urban League conferences, WriterCon, the Authors Marketing Guild, Houston's Writefest, Living Your Dreams Conference, the Marketplace Fair's Author Showcase, Houston Independent Authors' Writers Lunch, Nonfiction Authors Association, and the Houston Writers Guild. For more information about Sharon go to **www.supersuthorgranny.com** or **www.mcwritingservices.com**.

ABOUT THE AUTHOR

Philip Balonwu

Philip Balonwu is a visionary, philanthropist, and a man of many talents. He is a serial successful entrepreneur and media personality, with a Computer Science and Technical Management degree. He has worked as a Systems Engineer/ cloud architect in various industries with extensive experience in oil and gas, medical, finance, and IT sectors.

Mr. Balonwu founded Technology-Sure, an IT company that specializes in cloud architecture, web design, and cyber security. It is an IT company he founded to help bring technology to small businesses at affordable prices.

Due to his passion for media, he has dedicated his life to helping others and is a passionate advocate for the arts and music.

His love for promoting black culture worldwide led him to start Afrovibes TV & Radio Station in 2016, which is dedicated to promoting African culture through music, entertainment, and art. The station broadcasts across Africa, Europe, and the United States. Afrovibes Radio helps spread the word about African culture and arts across the diaspora. His company, Afrovibes TV & Radio Station is a 24/7 worldwide streaming platform on ROKU TV, Amazon Fire TV, website, and Mobile APP, and has been providing entertainment to audiences around the world since the mid 2000's.

In 2021, Afrovibes TV & Radio Magazine was created as an extension of Afrovibes TV & Radio's mission to promote black culture around the world. It features articles about Africans living abroad making significant contributions in various fields such as business, entertainment, fashion design, etc., highlights businesses, brands, and artists, and displays great creative writing pieces, articles, and visuals! It is available through a digital link, print, and PDF document for group distribution.

In 2022, he expanded into the coffee business with Afrovibes Coffee, a coffee company that sources its beans directly from farmers around the world and produces Cold brew coffee and expanding into making Coffee liqueur. The company sells cold brew coffee wholesale to businesses and individuals around the world who want to support African farmers by purchasing their fair-trade products.

He also owns Afrovibes Entertainment Group—an entertainment group that manages events and produces music videos, films, plays, television shows, and other forms of media that promote African culture and heritage around the world.

As an entrepreneur, Mr. Balonwu has been a driving force behind all the projects under his purview, from Afrovibes TV & Radio to

Magazine to TechnologySure. He is also very passionate about helping new artists get started in their careers so that they can have a platform for their artistry to be heard by others. He believes that music has the power to change people's lives for the better, which is why he takes such an active role in supporting young artists.

Mr. Balonwu believes that Africa deserves better than it's gotten from other countries in terms of representation in media—and he's doing his part to change that by creating work that celebrates diversity and gives African people their due credit as global citizens who have contributed to humanity for centuries! His vision is to promote black culture worldwide through his platforms on radio, television, and magazines.

THERE IS MORE TO COME...

The winter of 2023 will be an exciting time for readers as they will get to experience a continuation of the Virtuous Woman Series with book two, The Warrior Queen of Dala Dynasty.

Stay tuned for more adventures with Queen Zara, E., the Alagabatas, and Ropo! There is a Civil War brewing in Dala Dynasty, an upcoming wedding, and a major change in the royal hierarchy. You don't want to miss the preview of Chapter One which will be available in June 2023. Simply go to **www.superauthorgranny.com** and register for the Dala Dynasty News.

Happy Reading!

Check Out The New Song Inspired
By The Untold Love Story
By Rapper Rags: I Am Love

Get your copy on Spotify TODAY!

https://open.spotify.com/album/1sc4Ot4jxV0Fc25SE3ZqNQ